WITH THE FURY OF FLAME AND SHADOW

A MYTHOLOGICAL RETELLING

A. C. DAWN

CONTENTS

Notes from the Author: v

Prologue	1
Chapter 1	9
Chapter 2	16
Chapter 3	23
Chapter 4	31
Chapter 5	37
Chapter 6	46
Chapter 7	57
Chapter 8	63
Chapter 9	72
Chapter 10	80
Chapter 11	89
Chapter 12	102
Chapter 13	107
Chapter 14	117
Chapter 15	122
Chapter 16	127
Chapter 17	133
Also by A.C. Dawn	143
About A.C. Dawn	145

NOTES FROM THE AUTHOR:

I know that the Mesopotamian myths are not as well known as the Greeks and Norse. I had the opportunity a few years ago to ghostwrite a nonfiction retelling of the Mesopotamian, Babylonian, and Sumerian myths. I found them fascinating, but one in particular stuck out, The Marriage of Ereshkigal and Nergal. It was so unique among Underworld myths, particularly because of its strong female ruler.

A few things before we launch into the story. First of all, these myths have many versions since they come from the most the ancient of the ancient civilizations. They conquered each other constantly, which meant the conquering nation brought with them a new set of beliefs. Consequently, their myths went through several evolutions, resulting in gods and goddesses being consolidated or forgotten altogether. Gods and goddesses also have many different names. I've chosen the ones I like to use and stick to them to avoid confusion. Largely written on cuneiform tablets, the records of these myths were heavily damaged, which leaves the interpretations open to debate by scholars way smarter than me! I do strive to keep most of the cannon of the myth intact in my retellings, but since this is a fictional story, I take creative license to twist things around a bit!

With that said, here's a rundown of some of the key gods and goddesses in the Mesopotamian/Sumerian pantheon that play a role in this story.

Anu- He is the father god; god of all creation. He's the boss of the world.

Enki- The God of Wisdom and brother to Ereshkigal and Ishtar. He's second in command for the most part and very powerful.

Ereshkigal- The Goddess of the Underworld. She's the Queen of the Dead and daughter of Anu. In many versions, she's granted domain over the Underworld or Irkalla, as they called it. In the earlier myths, she rules sovereign and alone. In later myths, she becomes the wife of Nergal, God of War, and rules with him. Eventually, she disappears from the Underworld myths completely and Nergal becomes the sole ruler of the Underworld.

Ganzir- Ereshkigal's palace in the Underworld

Gugalanna- The Great Bull of Heaven. He is referenced quite a bit in the myths. He appears in his beast form when he lays waste to the town of Uruk under the control of Ishtar in the Epic of Gilgamesh (the most famous myth from Mesopotamia). He is also often described as Ereshkigal's husband and his death is the impetus for the second most famous myth, The Decent of Ishtar. I reference both of these myths in the story, and they are both worth looking up! The way I think about it is he's a giant bull but can also assume human form. Otherwise, it's just too confusing.

Irkalla- another name for the Underworld

Ishtar- The Goddess of Love. She's also known as the goddess of war, lust, sex, and justice. She's Anu's daughter and is incredibly powerful, cunning, and selfish. You might know her by the name Inanna as well. She's frequently called the Queen of Heaven, but her power and rule are secondary to Anu's.

Kur- This name sometimes refers to the Underworld and is also a mountain range in the ancient texts. In an old translation that has been debunked as false, they claimed Kur was a dragon who tried to steal the sun. When he couldn't, he stole Ereshkigal instead and trapped her in the Underworld. This is the version I used in my story, even though it isn't the most factual! (Kur the dragon is way more interesting than Kur the mountain range!)

Namtar-Ereshkigal's son in some versions and in others he is a messenger god who can travel between the planes. He is a minor god of death. In this story, he is the son of Ereshkigal and her first husband, Gugalanna

Nergal- The God of War and Pestilence. He's the balance to harmony in the universe. Without strife, happiness cannot be appreciated. Therefore, he is a necessary component in the concept of balance that ruled the ancient myths.

Shamash- The God of the Sun. He's usually fairly neutral in the myths but does lend a hand to heroes now and again.

Fictional characters:

Belanum- I created him to take the place of Kaka, a messenger for Anu. Honestly, I just couldn't have a character named Kaka!

Jazaroon- Demon bodyguard to Ereshkigal. She is entirely fictional but is one of my favorite characters in this story!

Hulla- Human who lives at the gates of Irkalla on the mortal side. She is clever, practical, and devoted.

I also use flowing praises and descriptive titles for the gods. This is very common among these myths. Sometimes the accolades, particularly to Anu, go on for pages worth of translation before you even get to what the person wants to say to him! I didn't get that carried away, but I included some to preserve the flavor of their speech.

Welcome to a forgotten world where gods and man walked side by side in the infancy of civilization. Enjoy the adventure of Ereshkigal, Queen of the Dead, Mistress of Darkness, and Goddess of the Underworld. I hope she captures your imagination and your heart as she did mine.

A.C. Dawn

PROLOGUE

The world teetered on the brink of war because of me, and it wasn't the first time.

Long ago, I lived in the world above with the other gods and goddesses. Newly created by the Great Father, Anu, the world revealed endless mysteries and wonders. A kaleidoscope of colors and experiences greeted us every day. In the age of creation, anything was possible.

When Enki, the god of wisdom, and the mother goddess, Ninmah, brought forth the race of man, the shape of the mortal plane changed but lost none of its splendor. From the moment of their creation, humans fascinated me. Simple yet resilient creatures, they learned quickly and possessed a passion for living. The gods taught the mortals to care for the earth, and themselves, and in return, they worshipped us.

The world, still in its infancy, had no defined realms, no boundaries. The gods populated the world with creatures—and monsters. From deep in the bowels of the earth, the mighty dragon, Kur, emerged. He brought forth the shadow realm, a place between darkness and light. He welcomed the monstrous creations and dark abominations made by the gods. Creatures of the shadows, they hid there, in the land between, watching the gods and mortals live their lives in the sun and grew jealous of the gods' powers.

The creatures of the shadow realm festered in their envy, adding layers of darkness amid the shadows of evil and anger. The shadow realm chafed under the brilliance of the world above until they could stand it no longer. Kur, fueled by the resentment of the dark, tried to steal the sun, but Anu had fixed it firmly in the sky. He even tried to swallow it, but it burned too hot.

The creator of the shadow realm was not so easily deterred. Forced to accept he would not have the sun, he sought something else to balance the realms, something that would light the darkness and remind the light of the shadow's power.

As the great dragon wrestled the sun, I swam in the cool river, naked and unafraid, watching and wondering if he would find success. His screams of frustration shook the earth, and his shadow blotted out the light. I glided through the cool water, floating on my back as Kur soared high above with his immense wings outstretched and his long sinuous body undulating as he cut through the sky.

He spotted me and landed next to the river with a thump that sent waves rolling through the water. Kur dangled his tail lazily in the current and watched me swim through the unsettled river. Sunning his iridescent scales, he stretched out on the riverbank with a long-suffering sigh.

"Why does Anu let his favorite daughter swim alone?"

I laughed and splashed water at the beast. "I'm not his favorite. Ishtar is, but I don't care. It pleases me to be able to swim, smell the sweetness of the flowers, and feel the sun on my skin."

Kur rumbled deep in his chest and his tail floated toward me, pulled by the gentle current. I darted away as it came close, and he raised it out of the water with a jerk and brought it back down, creating a massive wave. I dove beneath the water and caught the tip of his tail, tugging playfully. When I resurfaced, he slid into the water with me, wrapping his sinuous body loosely around me. The sun rippled along the water and Kur's scales glinted like gems.

"Would you like to feel the heat of the sun and the wind in your hair? Come, my beauty. Let me take you for a ride." His voice rumbled low and rasping.

In my childish innocence, I climbed onto his back, enchanted by his glittering scales. With every movement, they rippled and sparkled in the sun. The water heated around him, flowing like a hot bath over my legs. Goosebumps broke out on my shoulders and arms as the great beast swam with the current, casting waves high on the shore. I relaxed, laying back, and stared at the sky. The sun kissed my bare breasts and belly while Kur warmed my back. Delicious heat cocooned me until, with a mighty splash, Kur launched out of the water.

I sat up and gripped his sides with my legs. His wings beat and we climbed higher. I laughed at the joy of flying. My long black hair streamed behind me, and I threw my arms wide to feel the wind on my skin.

Enki saw us and demanded Kur bring me back, for he knew the dragon meant to keep me as his prize. Fear penetrated my euphoria when Kur laughed at the God of Wisdom and twisted in the air.

"If Anu will not share the great light with the world below, I will take Ereshkigal, Goddess of the Earth, to light the darkness and settle the balance, for what is above must be below." Kur's grating voice echoed across the land.

My fear escalated to terror as Kur dove into a dark cave that led to his lair. We twisted and turned in the dark, hurtling along through the cold, damp air.

Shivering, I pressed myself against Kur's back. I whispered my name on the wind and prayed to the Father of All that they would not forget me. Finally, in the space between the primordial waters at the heart of the world and the land above, Kur ceased his headlong flight. He skidded to a stop with a bone-jarring landing and tucked his wings into his body. I slid off his back and looked around the dark cavern.

No colors danced. No sunlight warmed my skin. Cold settled deep in my core as my vision adjusted to see the subtle shades of gray that ruled the world below.

"You will take me back," I demanded through clenched teeth. "I have no desire to live in this dark, cold place." I crossed my arms over my chest, hugging myself for warmth as shivers gripped me.

Kur merely shrugged. "Your desire means nothing, Ereshkigal. There must be balance between the realms. Once you cross into the world below, you may not leave without one to take your place. Is there someone who would trade their life in the sun for you?"

Many of my followers would be glad to serve and sacrifice themselves for me, though I would never doom another to such a fate. I held my silence and glared at Kur's insolence. I would have to trust my brother and father to find a way to free me.

Enki rallied the gods and mortals to fight for my freedom. They stormed across the sea and battered the entrance to Kur's lair with furious storms. The wind screamed through the warren of tunnels and the ground shook as the gods vented their displeasure.

Kur laughed and the creatures of the dark hissed and

roared in defiance. Kur gathered the demons, the shadow creatures, and the monsters of the deep. A hideous army of brute force and no morals, they rushed to meet the challenge. For days, the world trembled as gods and monsters battled. I watched in horror as mortals stood to defend me and fell under the thunderous onslaught. Finally, I could stand it no longer.

I put my voice on the wind and howled in desperation until both armies went still and silent.

"Anu, Father of all, hear me. I will stay in the world of shadows. Stop this fight." Tears coursed down my face as the wind carried my words and sealed my fate.

Anu, who had stood apart from the conflict, looked down from his heavenly throne and sadness filled his heart. He knew that after the gods and man experienced battle, they would never be the same. The earth bled with the devastation of the storms and the souls of the fallen mortals wandered, lost and abandoned. They had nowhere to go, for this was the first time the world had known death.

Anu stood between the armies. The shadow creatures hovered warily behind Kur, worried they would soon feel Anu's wrath. The weary gods and remaining mortals waited with anticipation for the Great Father to rescue his daughter and secure their victory.

"Since the day this world emerged from the primordial waters of the Abuz, I have sought balance. The universe demands this above all. Today, a restoration of balance is needed." The world held its breath as Anu turned to face Kur and his legions of shadow and darkness. "From this day forward, your realm is the Underworld. Its darkness balances the light and its power is of equal measure. My cherished daughter, Ereshkigal, shall rule this realm as your sovereign queen. I grant her the power of mortal death and the judgment of souls. The kingdom of Irkalla is hers and as is in heaven, so shall it be in the Underworld."

The proclamation echoed across the world as the earth shifted beneath our feet. My kingdom shaped itself at Anu's command, expanding Kur's shadowy domain. The souls of the fallen warriors bowed to me and streamed through the newly formed gates of the Underworld.

The creatures of the dark looked to Kur. He raised his chin in defiance. Anu rumbled his displeasure and lightning flashed across the sky. The creatures of the dark fled into the shadows. Kur nodded a mocking salute and followed them, his laughter echoing across the battlefields. With a sweep of his hand, Anu sealed the darkness beneath the earth and set the boundary for the Realm of the Dead. Resigned to my fate, I bowed to my father and turned toward my new home.

Enki fell into step beside me and walked with me to the first gate of Irkalla.

"You go into the darkness, sister, but do not hang your head. You are a goddess of the Earth and a daughter of the Great Father. You have more power than you know and carry enough light to banish even the darkest night. You must embrace the darkness before you can wield it." He kissed my brow, and I bowed to him, hearing little of his words through my misery. He shook his head and frowned at me. "Remember my words, Queen Ereshkigal. For one day, you will need them."

I bowed to him again, as was his due. My throat closed tight on words I couldn't speak so I smiled and walked through the main gate of Irkalla, leaving my life in the light behind.

I sighed, remembering that long ago day as I surveyed my army. I would claim more souls before this day was done, though the thought gave me no joy. Eager to fight, demons and furies wove among the dead, stirring bloodlust and hysteria among the host as they waited for my command.

Mother Goddess, how I wished Anu had never sent me that invitation. None of this would have happened. I would be sitting on my throne with Namtar's stories entertaining me, maybe even making me laugh. I would be blissfully ignorant of Nergal, the God of War, the god of arrogance, the god with jade green eyes and unruly black hair. The god who stole my heart and threw it away without a backward glance.

CHAPTER ONE

"She never smiles."
 I heard the comment, though it wasn't meant for my ears. My son huddled in the corner with Jaz, whispering about me and my mental state.

I sighed and pushed to my feet, unable to bear their concerned glances and worried whispers. I didn't know what they expected. As the queen of the dead, damned, and discarded, what did they think I had to smile about? The shadow realm held no levity, no color, no joy- nothing to lift the corners of my mouth into a smile.

Born in the space between worlds, Jazaroon and Namtar knew little of life in the sun, of colors so brilliant they hurt your eyes, and wide-open sky that testified to the infinity of the universe. Though time had eroded my memories to vague impressions, I knew the world held more than the dark underbelly we called home.

Shades and shadows rustled as I left the great hall to roam the vast warren of tunnels beneath the palace. When he named me queen of this realm, Anu insisted that everything my sister, Ishtar, had as the Queen of Heaven, I would have in equal measure. I had a grand palace, a court, and ultimate sovereignty of the realm. Ganzir, my palace, sat at the base of the great staircase that led to the mortal world in a mirror image of Ishtar's heavenly home.

Despite my father's intentions, Irkalla could never be the same as heaven. Instead of an infinite sky, glowing marble that radiated warmth, and the vast expanse of the vibrant world below it, Ganzir sat below a canopy of utter blackness that swallowed all light. It stole all color, ingesting it to feed the shadows. Cold gray stone made the palace walls while jagged rocks and tunnels full of shadows and creatures of darkness surrounded the castle. Through the heart of the kingdom, a sluggish river flowed both ways, a true testament to the contrary nature of Irkalla.

I ground my teeth together as I fought with bitter resentment that threatened to consume me. I walked faster, ignoring the scattering shadows as my feet pounded against the stone. The mockery of this kingdom, though unintentional, fed the jealousy that twisted in my gut. Distant memories of the heavenly court played in my mind. Gods, goddesses, magical creatures, and mortals wore robes of the finest weave with colorful tassels and gleaming gold and silver adornments. Food, beer, and wine flowed in abundance as feasts and celebrations entertained the court. They told stories, laughed, and sang. They made love under the stars and welcomed the sun and its warmth every morning.

In Irkalla, my court hid in pockets of shadows and pits of darkness or wandered in the endless tunnels. Some of them clustered in Ganzir's great hall, spirits of nobles, shades of warriors, and ghosts of common folk mixed with demons and creatures too foul to name as they rode out eternity within the walls of the dark palace. Together, they made up the host of Irkalla.

The luckier souls, whose families paid homage to the realm, had clothes of gray coarse fabric, water to drink, and meat to eat. Most wandered naked, cold and shivering, through the eternal gloom. They ate mud and drank dust. Silence reigned, punctuated by weeping and wails of the tormented. We spoke in whispers lest we wake the creatures that lurked in the dark. Time passed with excruciating slowness. The host quarreled, ate, and slept, but most of all, they watched the living with envy coursing through them. Such was our grand existence in the Underworld.

I ran my fingers over the rough stone of the tunnel wall. Fire light from ever-burning torches flickered and beat back some of the darkness, but I walked forward unseeing, uncaring of what might be lurking in the shadows. Frustration, grief, and anger surged through me. I clawed at the rock, breaking my nails back to the quick. I beat on the stone with my fists until my skin bled and a hint of pain penetrated my misery. Namtar's comment echoed in my ears. Smiling in the face of Irkalla's darkness had always been difficult, but ever since my husband's murder, I found it impossible.

Unbidden tears welled and spilled over as a fresh wave of grief gripped my heart. Since my sweet Gugalanna's death, time had passed as one long, dark blur. His visits had interrupted this interminable existence with pinpricks of light and levity and in their absence, I drifted as lost as the souls I ruled.

Anu created Gugalanna, the Great Bull of Heaven, a sweet, simple creature to comfort and warm me in my dark exile. As a divine creature who Anu granted a mortal form, he did not tally in the balance of souls and could travel freely between the realms. In his human form, Gugalanna brought news and stories from the land of the living.

Between visits, he grazed as a great beast in the heavenly pastures. He made me laugh and gave me my son. I missed him terribly. The wound in my heart refused to heal, and I found myself looking toward the stairs time and again, hoping he would emerge from the shadows.

Sliding down the rough stone, I scraped my back through my gown, though I barely felt it, numb as I was. I rested my forehead on my knees. My blood boiled afresh as I thought of his senseless death at my sister's hands.

"Come out, Jaz." I said, knowing she was near. She never let me out of her sight and hovered even closer in the wake of Gugalanna's death.

Silent as the shadows, she crouched next to me, her human façade in place over her demon. Strips of leather crisscrossed her chest, accentuating her breasts beneath her black tunic. A pair of wicked short swords hung in their scabbards on her back. More leather wrapped her forearms and her form-fitting black pants tucked into soft black boots. She wore her black hair twisted in intricate braids. Only her glowing red eyes interrupted the unrelenting black.

"Tell me the story again." I leaned my head back against the stone and closed my eyes, waiting for Jaz to tell me the tale of my husband's death.

Her disapproval of my request hung heavy in her answering silence.

"Tell me it again." I bit the words out, glaring at my only friend.

Jaz shook her head but sighed with resignation. "I see no point in recounting something you cannot change and causes you such grief. But I know you will not let it rest, so I will tell you one last time." She paused, frowning at me. I said nothing and lowered my head to my knees, waiting.

"King Gilgamesh of Uruk spurned Ishtar's advances

and her many offers for him to be her consort. Insulted, she demanded Anu allow her to take the Great Bull of Heaven to wreak havoc on the town in retribution. The Great Father refused, but Ishtar threatened to decimate the world by destroying the gates of Irkalla." Jaz growled low in her chest at the audacity of Ishtar to use the army of the dead like they were her own. "Anu gave her Gugalanna. She led him in his beast's form from his heavenly pastures. As Ishtar intended, he wreaked havoc on the city of Uruk. He drained the rivers and, with his hooves, gouged furrows in the land that swallowed hundreds of men."

I bit my lip, choking on my fury as I imagined Ishtar watching it all in delight from the city walls. My sweet Gugalanna, a pawn in her game. A beast of the heavens, he was never meant to roam the earth in that form. He knew nothing of the devastation he wrought. I leaned my head back against the stone of the tunnel and stared into the darkness beyond the weak torchlight.

Jaz continued with her story. "Instead of beseeching Ishtar for her help as she had intended, King Gilgamesh and his trusted companion, Enkidu, attacked the Great Bull and killed him." Jaz's voice held no more inflection than it had the first time she told me the story of Gugalanna's death. "As the bull fell, Ishtar stood on the walls of Uruk and watched in disbelief as his blood filled the rivers. The brave Enkidu flung a haunch at Ishtar and hit her in the face. At Anu's command, Ishtar led the women of Uruk in mourning for the Great Bull."

I blew out a long breath, remembering the moment I felt his soul part from his body. In his beast form, his awareness was scattered and confused. I wailed my grief, shaking the walls of Ganzir, as his simple soul blundered through the lands, seeking refuge until he followed the call of Irkalla.

"You could have kept him with you," Jaz said, surprising me. She had never mentioned my choice to turn him away.

Fresh tears fell as I thought of Gugalanna's bewildered pain, wanting to come to me, but finding his way blocked. I relieved Neti, the gate keeper, of his duties and stood guard at the first gate as my love begged for entrance, calling for me in his confusion. As he pounded on the gate, it tore holes in my heart, but I could not sentence my husband to an eternity in the darkness. He was a creature of the heavens and did not belong in Irkalla.

I shook my head. "No, Jaz. His misery at never seeing the stars or feeling the light on his face would have driven him mad. I could not endure that."

Anu had heard my grief echoing across the land. He set Gugalanna in the stars to dwell as the Great Bull, and my heart felt a little lighter knowing that he would burn with light for eternity.

Jaz nodded her understanding before adding, "I would have liked to see that haunch hit Ishtar in the face."

That brought a hint of a smile to my face, but it was short-lived.

"Leave me for now, Jaz. I'll come back to the palace shortly," I said and wiped my face with my hands.

Jaz stood and looked down at me for a long moment. I waited for her to tell me I needed to move on from my grief or to act like the queen I was. But she said nothing. She rested her hand on the top of my head for a moment before disappearing into the darkness.

I stood, but instead of following Jaz, I wandered deeper into the tunnels. I wrestled with the void left in my heart, trying to let go of my rage and grief. A wailing moan chased me down the passage and fluttered my silver-white hair as it passed. More souls to sort; more mouths to feed; more despair to fill the endless pit of hopelessness that anchored our existence. It would never end, and the weight of that smothered me.

I turned toward the pitiful sound and screamed until I had no breath. I sent my grief into the deserted darkness, echoing the wail of the dead. How much longer could I exist in the house of death without succumbing to it myself?

CHAPTER TWO

"My queen," a raspy voice came from the shadows.

My mood dipped from bad to worse. The normal-looking rock suddenly displayed golden eyes as a sinewy body unwound from what had appeared solid stone. Black scales shimmered as they caught the torchlight.

"Kur. What are you doing here?" I asked, folding my arms across my chest in an ineffectual barrier against the creature who sentenced me to this miserable existence.

He huffed, stirring dust in the tunnel. "I do not need a reason to seek my queen." His tail curled around me and pushed me toward him.

"Your queen? That implies loyalty and obedience. I've observed neither from you," I snapped as I twisted out of his grasp and hopped over his tail.

Despite my loathing and repeated reprimands, Kur persisted in inflicting his presence on me. He infiltrated the tunnels, my palace, and even my bedroom with annoying regularity. Though I ruled this domain, as the creator, Kur held the power to go anywhere he wanted, and he didn't take no for an answer.

A low growl rumbled through the tunnel in response to my rebuff and a rush of wind extinguished the torch. I froze in the sudden darkness, waiting, listening. Fear rose in my chest. Had that been the dragon, or was there something else in the tunnel with us?

By my order, torches continuously lit the tunnels and the palace. Kur was only one of many of the dark creatures in the realm, and not the worst by far. The shadow creatures that once obeyed him had grown in strength and numbers, eroding Kur's dominance. While I had no love for the dragon, he kept the fearsome monsters in check, but with his control slipping, the darkness held danger, even for me. The title of queen meant nothing to a creature of shadow that fed on evil and despair.

Kur's jagged voice whispered in the darkness. "You refuse me? You, who accepted the Great Bull and bore his child, turn away from me, time and time again?"

In the utter blackness, he circled around me. His smooth scales slid across my skin. My heart galloped as panic shot through me. For centuries, he'd tormented me like this. In the wake of Gugalanna's death, Kur's visits increased. Every time he touched me, I relived the terror of hurtling through the darkness into the shadow realm and mourned the loss of the light in my life.

I despised him and that he could still make me feel like a naive goddess happy to climb on his back so he could abduct me. I had no innocence left, and I refused to show weakness no matter how my stomach clenched or my heart knocked in my chest. Instead of calling for Jaz and her guard, I raised my chin and donned my queenly airs, fighting my resentment for the title.

"I do not justify my choices to you or any other creature. Leave, beast, and do not return unless I call for you— which I can assure you will never happen." My voice rang with confidence, though my hands shook.

Kur's laugh, low and thunderous, echoed around me. "Such a queen." He mocked me. "I have something for you."

"There is nothing you have that could interest me. Leave—now."

I gasped as he tightened his long, powerful body around me. In his grip, I stood like a statue as he sighed with contentment. Aggravated, mainly with myself, I commanded the torches to relight. The tunnel flooded with a brilliant flash, far more than I had called for. Kur evaporated in the brightness, and I covered my face with my hands. When the light dimmed, I looked around, blinking as I tried to clear the spots from my vision. Kur had vanished, but a man stood silhouetted in the torch light.

He moved toward me with a graceful prowl. Freshly oiled, his ebony skin gleamed beneath the robe that hung open, exposing his muscular chest. He smiled, and white teeth flashed in the firelight. I stared at him in wonder. This was not a soul, dead or damned, and mortals could not walk the halls of Irkalla in their fleshly bodies.

"Who are you?" I demanded, torn between curiosity and fear. Part of me wondered if the darkness had finally broken my mind, and I imagined this creature before me.

"Do you not know me, my queen?" Kur's unmistakable voice answered. He closed the distance between us and looked down at me with familiar golden eyes.

My mouth went dry as I stared up at him. His beauty stole my breath. I tried to reconcile this man with the dragon I despised. In all the centuries, he had never revealed this form to me, and his exquisite perfection left me speechless.

Kur raised his hand and traced his fingers down my cheek. I should have batted it away. I should have called the furies to chain him in the fiery depths of Irkalla for touching me. I should have screamed, or kicked, or clawed his eyes out. I shouldn't have sighed and leaned into the hand that cupped my face. I couldn't help it. He was warm, full of radiating heat, and I wanted to wrap myself in it.

Kur's golden gaze sharpened, and his smile widened at my reaction. He pulled his hand away and crossed his arms over his chest. The cold air felt even colder in the absence of his touch, and bitter resentment rose in my chest. This was the Kur I knew— cruel, tormenting beast.

I drew myself up and mirrored his posture. I wasn't an innocent child swimming in the river anymore.

Before I could speak, he announced, "I want to marry you, Ereshkigal, Queen of the Damned, Beauty of the Darkness."

Kur's blunt statement stole my words and intention. I sucked in a surprised breath and answered automatically, "I will never marry again."

Kur's eyes flashed with golden flames at my refusal. He circled me once again, walking with slow, measured steps.

"A queen needs a mate. A woman needs a man. You're fading, Ereshkigal. Losing yourself to the gray and black shadows, becoming one of the wretched wraiths you're supposed to rule. You need fire back in your soul."

He halted his spiraling circle to stand behind me, drawing his hands up my arms and pulling me back against him.

I swallowed my protests as his solid warmth enveloped me. Though I hated myself for it, I leaned against him. My mind succumbed to the inferno of desire that rose within me. It had been so long since someone had touched me. Kur's hands roamed over my body, spreading trails of heat. His hot breath tickled my neck as he dipped his head to place a soft kiss against my shoulder. I shuddered in pleasure. His hand settled on my belly and anchored me against him.

"I have enough fire for both of us. I will keep you warm. You can reclaim the light you've lost." Kur's hand splayed across my midsection and liquid heat radiated through me. It filled me like flowing lava, leaving me burning with a desperate need for more. I closed my eyes and red, yellow, and orange flares of light danced behind my lids.

I jerked in Kur's embrace. I hadn't seen bright colors for longer than I could remember, even in my dreams. His low throaty chuckle rumbled as he trailed kisses up my neck and nibbled just behind my ear.

"This is just a sample of what I can do for you, my queen. Accept my offer and I will make you burn brighter than the sun."

Oh, I wanted to. I wanted this man and his fire. I wanted to take him within me and feast on his heat until I combusted. I wanted him to banish the dark and light my miserable life with his delicious caresses.

Intoxicated with heat and excitement, I parted my lips to tell him I wanted him to burn me to the ground when an ear-splitting shriek pierced the silence.

Jazaroon and her guard emerged from all sides. The furies blazed through the tunnel, alight with the ever-burning fire of the earth's core, and Jaz and her demons sported their true forms in all their hideous glory. Jaz tackled me, wrenching me away from Kur's embrace. In the absence of his heat, icy cold gripped me as my guard covered my body with hers.

Another flash of blinding light filled the tunnel. Demons and furies screamed and covered their eyes, dropping to the stone floor of the tunnel. A rush of wind washed over us before silence and darkness descended. For a heartbeat, nobody moved. Then Jaz rolled, pulling me to my feet with her and shouting orders. The torches flared back to life and demons set out in all directions in pursuit.

Jaz towed me along as my mind fought to find purchase in my tumbling thoughts. I almost agreed to marry Kur. Father Above, what kind of spell had he put me under? The memory of his heat, the hard planes of his body against mine, the touch of his kiss overrode the disbelief. More shocking yet, even as I followed Jaz into my chambers, I continued to consider the proposition.

Jaz slammed the door shut behind us and spun around to face me.

"Who was that? Why didn't you return to the palace? Did he hurt you?" She fired off her questions while her gaze raked me up and down. Still in her demon form, her words hissed out around her needle-like teeth. She pinned her leathery wings behind her. Her black skin, smooth but virtually impenetrable, absorbed the light from the fire as she loomed over me. She crossed her arms over her chest and her red eyes flashed. Her skeletal features appeared even more menacing in her displeasure. She shifted back to her human form but lost none of her intimidating presence.

"I'm fine, Jaz. I just needed some space and Kur was lurking down in the tunnels. I..."

Jaz cut me off. "That was Kur? I should have known that filthy son of a goat would come sniffing around. I'll double the guards. Gods, between him and the unrest among the fire giants, I'm running out of demons."

I didn't answer. The fire giants had been warring for eons. Every now and again, their wars erupted above the surface and the earth bled fire. We had no control over them but tried to keep their fighting away from Ganzir. Jaz frowned at my lack of response as I sat on a chaise, staring into the fire, lost in my thoughts.

"What in the name of Anu did he do to you?"

I reached toward the fire. It crackled and danced at my command, but I couldn't feel its heat. I thrust my hand into the flames and didn't even feel a twinge of warmth. The thought of the molten heat Kur had ignited in me made me bite my lip as I withdrew my hand. I looked at my uninjured skin and sighed, wondering what to do.

Jaz stomped over, placing herself between me and the fire.

I held up my hand to forestall her lecture. "I wasn't in any danger, Jaz. Kur wouldn't hurt me."

"It's not Kur I'm worried about," she snapped. "Neti sent word. There's a visitor at the gate."

CHAPTER THREE

I shot to my feet. "Is it Ishtar? Has she come with more tricks?" I demanded as I headed for the doors to my chambers.

In the wake of the Great Bull's death, Ishtar came to Irkalla under the pretense of offering her condolences. In her monumental arrogance, she tried to seize my throne, seeking to couple the power of the underworld with that of heaven. As always, she underestimated me. The last time I smiled was when I struck my sister down and tacked her hide to the wall in the great hall of Ganzir.

Of course, Ishtar was no fool. She planned for an escape before entering Irkalla. She offered her lover, Dumuzid, to take her place. Regretfully, once the demons returned with the unfortunate Dumuzid, I had to let Ishtar leave. Such were the laws of the universe. In the wake of her infiltration, the realm remained unsettled, and Neti, the gatekeeper, maintained high alert.

Jaz caught my arm and pulled me to a stop. "Slow down. Neti has the gates secured and is waiting to discuss it further. When he announced the visitor and no one could find you, well...," she trailed off.

I nodded. With everyone on their guard, they had immediately assumed abduction or assassination and responded accordingly.

"Well, let's hear what Neti has to say. Then, we can decide on how to welcome our guest." I pulled my arm free of Jaz's grip and led the way to the hall where Neti and Namtar stood talking in urgent whispers. They fell silent as we approached.

"Get out!" Jaz's voice roared. With a loud rustle and sigh, the shades scattered at her command.

"Was that necessary?" I asked as I sat on my plain stone throne and gave Jaz a disapproving look. The host was skittish at the best of times. They would hide in the shadows for days in their present agitation.

Jaz shrugged. "Made me feel better." She assumed her post just behind my right shoulder. "They needed a little stirring up. Some of them hadn't moved in a week."

I shook my head and took a deep breath, trying to focus my thoughts that still strayed to my strange encounter with Kur and his unbelievable proposal.

"Who is this visitor, Neti?" I asked and gestured for him and Namtar to join me.

Neti bowed before answering, "My queen, a man, who claims to be a messenger from your father, waits at the gate. He calls himself Belanum and bears a scroll with the heavenly seal."

"I think we should let him in. Even if he has ill intent, we cannot allow ourselves to hide behind a locked gate. We can handle anything they might send." Namtar added his opinion. My son was always quick to defend any possible slight against Irkalla.

I considered for a moment. I didn't doubt Ishtar would steal Anu's seal, but her last trip to Irkalla left her in poor standing with the rest of the gods—not that she cared. Ishtar cared only for herself and her desires. However, only a fool would openly defy the entire heavenly court when she stood in disgrace and Ishtar was no fool. She may be the Queen of Heaven in title, but much of her power depended on the good favor of our father and the other gods. I very much doubted Ishtar would cross them again with such a blatant ploy.

This visitor could be a ruse by a new enemy, someone no less cunning than my sister to have stolen the heavenly seal. However, Namtar had a point. Whoever waited at the gate, the strength of Irkalla could not be allowed to fall into question.

"Neti, bring our guest to me." I held up a hand to silence Jaz, who was already hissing in my ear. "I hear you, Jaz, but I will not hide in the darkness. Send a guard with Neti. Let us see who has come knocking."

Neti bowed and hurried out of the chamber with Jaz on his heels, issuing commands. I sighed and waited, swinging from excitement to dread and back again. What had happened that would cause my father to send a message? Could Ishtar possibly be desperate enough to attempt another coup after failing so badly last time? Impatiently, I pushed to my feet to pace around the empty hall. Namtar said nothing, but his gaze tracked my every footstep.

"This is no way to receive the emissary of Anu. Take your hands, or whatever those are, off me." A shrill, angry voice cut through the silence.

Namtar chuckled. "It seems Jaz is giving him an Irkalla welcome."

I couldn't help the grin that spread on my lips as I

reclaimed my throne to receive the visitor. "Let's just hope she hasn't damaged him. I doubt Anu would be amused."

The doors to the hall burst open and several demons swarmed through in front of Jaz, who in full demonic glory, dragged a thin man along beside her. His sandals slapped the stones as he stumbled to keep up with her long strides. When they stopped before the dais, the man wrenched his arm away from my bodyguard, straightening his shoulders and smoothing his robes. He ran a hand over his oiled black hair and beard. With a regal air, he approached my throne and dropped to his knees. He pressed his forehead to the rough stone and waited for me to acknowledge him. This man certainly knew his etiquette, though in Irkalla, we did not observe such strict rules.

"Rise," I snapped, eager to hear his news and impatient with his pomp.

"I am Belanum," the messenger announced in his nasally tones as he rose gracefully to his feet.

Why would my father choose someone with such an irritating voice to be a messenger? I forced myself not to flinch and nodded to the man.

"I bear a message from the great Father of All. Anu, he who is full of light and blessing, he who created the world above and below, he who—"

"State your message and save the praises for the heavenly court," Jaz growled, cutting the recitation of my father's many godly attributes short.

Belanum glared at Jaz. "Filthy creature. You know nothing of etiquette. The Great Anu, who gave even a creature such as you life, deserves all praise."

I raised a brow. Few men would call Jaz a filthy creature to her face. Even less would live to tell the tale, but she would not strike down the ingratiating little man without my permission.

Jaz bared her needle-sharp teeth and her demonic eyes flared red. As the demon towered over him, Belanum swallowed hard and his breath caught.

With a display of common sense that surprised me, the messenger hurried to say, "Anu sends his blessing to you, Queen Ereshkigal, Queen of the Underworld, Ruler of the Dead, and Mistress of the Darkness." He bowed again, but just a simple bend at the waist. He straightened and stood waiting with his eyes cast down at the stone floor, though he flicked uneasy glances toward Jaz, who stood with a short sword gripped in her hand.

I glanced around the chamber full of demons and darkness. They all watched intently for the smallest indication of threat. Belanum appeared to be exactly what he claimed to be. As a heavenly messenger, he, like Namtar, could travel between the realms. Excitement skittered through me. In all the years since I walked through the gates of Irkalla, my father had never once sent me a message.

"Welcome to Irkalla, Belanum. I confess this message from my father surprised us. You will forgive our caution after my sister's recent visit."

Belanum nodded and his mouth twisted in distaste. "Lady Ishtar's violation of this kingdom is regrettable, and your father has forbidden any further interference. The mighty Anu, Father of light, Master of—" Belanum swallowed the rest of his litany of praises when Jaz growled low in her chest. His already squeaky voice sounded even more pinched as he hurried on, "Anu wishes me to give you this message and convey his deepest affection for you."

When Belanum reached into his robe, Jaz tensed and tightened her grip on her sword. The messenger stepped forward but froze in his tracks when the sharp edge of Jaz's sword snapped up, barring his way. I frowned at her, but she ignored me. Another low, guttural growl rumbled through her chest and several of her guards edged in closer. Namtar hurried forward to retrieve the scroll and inspected it quickly. When he handed it to me, Jaz lowered her sword and Belanum crossed his arms over his chest, shooting an irritated glance at my demonic guard.

I unrolled the scroll, trying not to appear overeager, and Namtar peered over my shoulder. Belanum's eyes widened with shock at the utter disregard for courtly protocol. My eyes widened in a similar fashion as I read the message.

Queen of Irkalla, Mistress of Darkness, Goddess of Death, Queen among Shadows...

I skimmed over several more lines of praises, though the last one caught my eye.

My cherished daughter,

I am hosting a banquet in your honor. While I know you cannot attend, I urge you to send an emissary who can accept the hospitality and comfort of my court. It saddens me that I cannot look upon you, but I hope that the honor I pay you will warm your heart and remind you of your father's affection.

I wish you happiness, warmth, and light from the one who gives blessings, from the bringer of light, from the Father of All...

I didn't read the next several inches of writing listing Anu's many attributes. In stunned silence, I stared at the words until it blurred as my thoughts spun in a dozen different directions. Ishtar's infiltration of Irkalla must have angered my father profoundly to prompt such an outreach. I examined the seal. Though I had not seen it in a very, very long time, I recognized the intricate fan shape covered in stars suspended over the sun. It reflected his supremacy over all things and his all-encompassing vastness. As unbelievable as it was, this message came from my father.

I sighed. Even the master of all creation could not overcome the laws of the universe. The land of the living and the land of the dead must stay in perfect balance. Despite Anu's greatness, he could not give me even a day in the sun without tipping that balance. The thought of walking among the living with the sun's warmth kissing my face and colors filling my vision sent a pang of longing through me and brought Kur's unholy proposition to mind.

I pushed the scroll into Namtar's hand and stood up. Belanum dropped to his knees, keeping his eyes averted. The demons looked at him like he had lost his mind. I ground my teeth together, suddenly aggravated with the entire situation.

"Get up," I barked at Belanum. "In the house of the dead, we do not grovel." The messenger scrambled back to his feet, but kept his face turned deferentially away from me. At least he was off the floor. That would have to be enough, especially since he was leaving immediately. "Namtar will accompany you to the banquet and receive all due honors in my name." I made the announcement even as my heart squeezed with the unfairness of it all.

Namtar, reading my mood and undoubtedly excited about a trip to the land of the living, hurried forward. As a creature born between the realms, Namtar did not count in the balance and could move freely between the land of the living and the dead. He rarely had cause to leave Irkalla, but I could see the eagerness in his eyes. I smiled. At least my son could escape this gloomy existence.

"I will serve you well, Mother. All who gather will

know your power and grace," Namtar said, tapping into his natural smooth-talking charisma.

"Travel safely, my son. I look forward to hearing about your adventure." I forced my smile to stay in place, though a pang of jealousy ate through my gut. I wanted to accept Anu's gifts for myself. I wanted one day out of this wretched darkness. But as Namtar and Belanum left the hall, I ruthlessly pushed my petty envy away.

I felt Jaz's gaze and met her eyes, hoping my façade of the serene queen would fool her. I doubted it did, but she didn't follow as I fled to my chambers.

CHAPTER FOUR

I drew up short when I entered my room and found a man sprawled on the chaise near the fire. His ebony skin glistened in the fire light and his golden gaze met mine with a smoldering desire. He wore a loin skirt slung low across his hips with his torso bare, exposing sculpted muscles across his belly, shoulders, and chest.

Armed with irritation and general aggravation with the world, Kur's beauty and obvious offer held no temptation for me.

"Get out," I growled and crossed my arms over my chest.

"Don't growl at me, Ereshkigal. I'm not the one you're mad at."

Even though I knew they would have as much impact as a raindrop against rock, I let my words tumble out, gaining heat with every syllable.

"You're right, Kur. I'm not mad at you. I left my anger behind centuries ago. All I'm left with is my cold, constant hatred of you. I will never forget that your selfish greed caused every moment of my misery. Anger is a flickering flame, but the loathing I feel for you burns as eternal as the sun. Now, get out before I seal you into the deepest pit I can find and let you spend eternity digging yourself out."

Power rolled through me as I let my emotions flow and tapped into long forgotten powers given to all gods. Stuck in the shadows beneath the living, my powers lay dormant, unneeded and unused. I used the power of death to pass judgement, sort the souls who flocked to Irkalla, and dole out rewards or punishments. I did not need to channel the flowing power of the earth and sky. Routine and monotony had stolen the opportunity or desire to do anything more than go through the drudgery of my tasks.

Now, I took a deep breath and towered over Kur, surprised and excited as the energy answered my call. Mother Goddess, help me. The power made my head spin and heart hammer as it coursed through me. When was the last time I'd wielded the might of the gods?

Kur's white teeth flashed in a smile as he got to his feet. "Ah, there's the queen."

He reached toward me, but I slapped his hand away. Kur raised an eyebrow and gave a shrug.

"As you wish, my lady. It's too bad you're missing the banquet. I bet Ishtar will enjoy herself immensely." He turned and ducked into the fire, dissolving into flame.

Kur's parting jab struck home. He had a point. If Ishtar was in my position, she would attend the banquet, even if it meant upsetting the balance of the world. I pressed my lips together as I paced in front of the fire, balling my hands into fists. I wasn't a selfish, power monger like my sister. I honored my word and would not lower myself to her standards.

An idea germinated in the back of my mind. It started as a whisper, and though I tried to ignore it, grew louder and louder until I couldn't hear the reasons I should stay forever doomed to this dismal world.

I whirled around and ran. If I hurried, I could catch them before they made it to the main gate. Kur's laughter echoed around me as I rushed through the tunnels.

I flew through the seven gates, leaving them yawning on their hinges. Their demon sentinels scrambled to close them in my wake. I plowed through newly arrived souls as they plodded downward to Ganzir's great hall to receive their final judgement.

Today, they would have to wait. For once, I was taking control of my destiny.

"Namtar, wait," I called as I raced up the stone stairs to the last gate that separated the living and the dead.

Namtar stopped and turned, drawing the knife at his belt, and scanning the area for threats. Neti raised the alarm, shrieking a cry that caused the dead to cower in the shadows. He lowered the massive bar across the gate with a resounding thud and drew his sword, setting his feet ready for a fight.

Behind me, Jaz and her demons thundered toward us, responding to the call. Souls swarmed everywhere, trying to stay out of the way, but unsure of where to go or what to do. Some tried to run, while others froze in place. They jammed together on the staircase, but I vaulted over them as I pelted toward Namtar and Belanum.

I tackled Belanum without breaking stride and rolled to pin him to the stone stairs. Namtar dropped to his knees and pressed his blade to the messenger's throat.

"Say the word and he will die for whatever insult he paid you." My son's face darkened with murderous rage.

I covered his hand with mine and withdrew the blade.

"Let me up. This is outrageous. Your father will hear

about this," Belanum shrieked as he twisted and squirmed beneath me.

I glared at him and let the power of death rise within me. My face transformed to a skeletal visage. The dark pits of my eyes reflected the emptiness of the eternal void as I stared at Belanum. He went still and whimpered, squeezing his eyes shut.

"Please, have mercy. I beg you." His words shook and his lips trembled.

I pushed away from the terrified man and stood, once again assuming my fully fleshed appearance. Jaz and her guard arrived, and dozens of blades, claws, and fangs hovered ready to meet the threat. Belanum curled into a ball and mumbled a disjointed prayer to Anu. It was a waste of breath. Even my father's almighty gaze couldn't penetrate Irkalla's darkness.

"Put away your arms. There is no need for them. As you can see, he poses no threat."

The demons reluctantly stood down, looking disappointed and confused. Jaz set her hands on her hips, and Namtar gazed up at me with concern in his eyes.

"I will attend this banquet in my honor. You," I nudged Belanum with my toe, "will stay below to balance the planes. Come, my son. We must not be late for my celebration." I smiled at him and held out my hand.

Jaz was in front of me in a blur of motion, trampling the heavenly messenger, who squeaked like a mouse and curled tighter into himself.

"You can't march into the heavenly court on a whim. I need time to prepare and will have to go ahead of you to make sure it's safe—not to mention reinforce the guard here. Ishtar will not hesitate to steal your throne without you here to secure it," my bodyguard reminded me, as she crossed her arms over her chest and stubbornly set her feet.

Namtar stood but didn't take my hand. His expression clouded with uncertainty as he looked from me to Jaz to the man on the ground.

Anger, hot and bright, flashed through me. Again, I let the face of death rise to the surface. Namtar immediately looked away as I leveled my gaze at him. Jaz narrowed her eyes in challenge, but after a moment, dropped her gaze to the stones at her feet. I rarely displayed my power, but lately it seemed like everyone needed a reminder that I ruled this realm.

"Jaz, take our guest to the hall. See to his needs and treat him like the honored emissary he is."

Jaz rolled her eyes and huffed in disapproval but gestured for a pair of demons to retrieve Belanum from where he cowered on the stones. She turned to lead her guard back to the hall, but I stopped her with a hand on her arm.

"He will be alive when I return."

I waited until she nodded stiffly before letting go. She retreated into the gloom without a backward glance. A pang of remorse cut through my excitement. Jaz took her duty very seriously and I had demoted her to a child minder. I would have to repair the breach in our friendship, but first, I planned to finish what I started.

Namtar smiled at me, mischief lighting his eyes. "What do you have in mind? Jaz is quite right about you marching into the heavenly court with all your deathly beauty on display. It will be chaos."

I took his offered arm and gestured for Neti to open the gates. I walked into the world above for the first time in forever. The sunlight kissed my skin and warm air engulfed me. I raised my face to the sun and my smile drew so wide it hurt. I drew in a deep breath, delighting in the fresh air.

I laughed, though it sounded strange to my ears. "I can smell the sunshine." I pulled Namtar away from the gateway of the dead and squeezed his arm. "Don't worry. I've got a plan."

CHAPTER FIVE

My euphoric sojourn into the light lasted only a few seconds before pain erupted as my skin burned and the sun overwhelmed my eyes, forcing me to squeeze them shut and clutch blindly to Namtar's arm. Anywhere the light touched, my skin cracked and blistered. Pain raced across my body. I covered my face with my hands, though they burned with pain like someone was flaying my skin from my bones.

Namtar pushed me into a shadowy outcropping near the entrance. He pulled my hands away from my face, and I cautiously peered up at him.

"Slow down, Mother. It's been a long time since you've been on this side of the gate. Let me arrange a few things for you. I'll be back in a moment." He dropped a kiss on the top of my head and hurried away.

Huddling back against the cool rock face, I tucked my toes under my robes and willed myself not to cry. Pain and bitter disappointment gripped me. I had imagined this moment countless times, though I hadn't thought of it in many years. I envisioned myself striding into the light that once baked my skin to a dark brown. The earth would know me and swirl a warm breeze to embrace me after all this time.

Now, here I was, cowering in the shadows, like a pitiful wraith. The undignified reality stole my dreams and ground them to dust. Despite my assurances to Namtar, I had no plan. I recognized the folly of my snap decision, but the thought of standing in the heavenly court with the gods cowering at my feet consumed me. I couldn't appear among the gods blistered and weeping, but death had taught me many lessons over the years and chief among them was patience. I would have my day in the sun.

I pulled in a deep breath. Warm air filled my lungs and soothed some of my angst. I rested my head against the rock and tried to blink away the spots dancing in my vision. I watched the souls of the dead milling about, oblivious to the world around them, as they made their way to Irkalla.

From my shadowy nook, I squinted against the sun's brightness and studied the expanse of barren sand that marked the entrance to the Underworld. In the distance, I saw the walls of a city and marveled. Over the shifting sands came noise from the bustling city. When I had descended to the Underworld, a small village sat in the distance with a temple and a few clusters of homes. Now a road, jammed with travelers moving in both directions, skirted the boundary to Irkalla and led to the thriving community. A small mud brick home stood on the edge of the road, standing sentinel near Irkalla's gate.

Namtar emerged from the hut with a woman carrying a bundle. They hurried toward me. The woman's eyes widened when she saw me huddling against the rock. She thrust the bundle into Namtar's hands and threw herself on the ground, pressing her forehead to the ground.

"Rise," I said, pulling myself into a more dignified position but staying safely away from the sun's touch.

The woman sat on her heels, but kept her eyes averted. Namtar introduced her as Hulla, the daughter of the mortal gatekeeper and one of Anu's high priests. Hulla smiled shyly, and I smiled back as I offered my hand. My ivory skin bore no sign of blisters or burns and I kept it carefully out of the light. Hulla pressed my hand to her forehead and murmured a prayer of gratitude and mercy.

Unsure of what to do next, I glanced at Namtar.

"Hulla has clothes and will dress you in the latest fashions. Believe it or not, Irkalla has not kept up with the new styles of the living."

Namtar's eyes sparkled as he teased. He shook out a billowing cloak and flung it around my shoulders, tugging the hood over my head. Protected from the sun, I followed him and Hulla toward the small hut. Shades and spirits shuffled toward the gate, though small clusters huddled along the side of the road. They called out piteously to us.

"Why do they not cross over? They are members of the dead and belong to me." It disturbed me that they could avoid the draw of Irkalla.

"Be gone!" Hulla waved her hand to clear them out of our path. "If you had lived honorable lives, you would not have to worry about crossing into the dark realm." The shades scurried away but did not make for the gate. Hulla made a disgusted noise. "They linger here, hoping they can convince their families to increase their offerings so you will have mercy on them. Shameful pigs." She spat on the sand.

"Do they bother you?" Namtar asked, glowering at the spirits.

"No, they don't interfere with me or my family as we do

our duties, but their moaning and crying is tedious," Hulla answered as we walked.

"Namtar, when this day is done, you will see to this. The dead belong among the host in Irkalla, not wandering about hoping to improve their lot. You will work with Neti to ensure this does not continue."

"Of course, Mother," Namtar replied as we reached the tiny courtyard around the mudbrick house.

I caught the look he exchanged with Hulla and guessed this was not Namtar's first visit to Hulla's hut. I wondered if Hulla had anything to do with Namtar's frequent visits to the first gate. He often insisted he needed to consult with Neti about something and would disappear for long stretches of time. If my mother's intuition was correct, Namtar sought far more than counsel on his trips to the entrance to the Underworld and I had just given him even more reason to come to the surface.

"You'll wait here. I will see to the queen." Hulla's low throaty voice halted Namtar at the entrance, and he grinned at her with a familiarity that added to my suspicions.

I focused my thoughts back to the business at hand as I followed Hulla inside. She pulled the cloak from my shoulders, hanging it on a peg. Bustling about, she seated me and filled a basin with water.

Hulla dropped to her knees and removed my sandals. She hummed under her breath as she washed my feet with reverence. She rubbed sweet oil over my skin, and I smiled down at her. I couldn't remember the last time anyone had paid me such sweet respect. In the land of the dead, such customs were superfluous.

I studied Hulla as she moved with efficient, confident grace. Her dark eyes brimmed with intelligence and her smile bore testament to the genuine goodness in her heart.

As the Goddess of Death, I could easily see her inner purity and selfless soul. She hummed as she brushed out my hair and rubbed oil over my skin. The sweet fragrance washed over me. I relaxed with my eyes closed, drinking in memories of swimming in clear, cool water under the blooming orchids.

"We have to cover your hair, my queen." Hulla murmured as she braided my white tresses in a complicated pattern around my head. She sighed as she ran her fingers over my hair. "It glitters like a gemstone."

I glanced at Hulla's long black braid. Long, long ago, my hair bore the same hue. After my countless years in the Underworld, my skin had faded from deep bronze to a pale ivory. Every garment I owned, regardless of the color or delicate weave of the fabric, faded to coarse gray cloth that chafed and hung without style or grace. The Underworld gobbled up any light or color that entered the realm, hoarding them to deepen the shadows.

"Do what you must, Hulla. I put my trust in you," I said, and tried to quell the riot of butterflies in my belly.

While Hulla fussed and primped, I distracted my anxious mind by recalling the names of colors. Red, yellow, blue, green. I remembered them, but so many more eluded me. The walls held vases of every hue and flowers and herbs overflowed from them, adding to the array of color. I concentrated on the colored crystals that adorned the altar place near the door. Emerald glimmered green and bright, reminding me of the leaves of the trees that grew near the river. A bloodstone, black with a bright red streak, stood prominently on display for protection. Lapis lazuli sparkled with deep blue and... I thought hard, seeking the deeper contrasting color. Indigo. The word popped into my mind, and I smiled.

"Indigo." I said it out loud to help remember it and enjoyed the feel of it on my tongue.

"Yes. It's one of my favorites. It would look beautiful against the silver of your hair and white skin," Hulla said with a wistful tone. "I wish I had a silk in that color. Unfortunately, my father does not believe in dressing with color, so I put it on the walls." She gestured at her colorful décor.

"It is no matter, Hulla. I am grateful for anything you can lend me."

My shortsightedness pained me. Ishtar would have never been caught in such a position, but I would not let minor obstacles like garments or colors stand in my way. I stood and Hulla draped a light brown robe around me, covering as much of my skin as possible with clever twists and folds. I refused to be disappointed that it wasn't indigo.

"It isn't the typical dress for the high court, but it won't stand out. May I make a suggestion?" Hulla asked as she knotted the robe snugly at my waist.

"Of course. I would welcome advice from a faithful daughter." I bowed my head so she could drape a matching scarf over my hair and cover my face with a sheer veil.

"As the daughter of a high priest, I have been to court to serve many times." She pulled two sparkling pins from her hair and tacked the veil in place. "If you attend in the glory of your true appearance, which is your right as a queen," she hurried to add. I smiled to encourage her to speak candidly. "You will disrupt the court, and the banquet will not go forth."

Namtar had said something similar, though I hadn't given it much thought. I imagined myself presiding over the banquet with my father to my left, Enki on my right, and Ishtar sitting on the floor like a dog at my feet. However, Hulla was correct. My sudden appearance would throw everything into turmoil. Enki would worry about the balance of the planes. Ishtar would screech and tear at her hair over some contrived insult and stir the gods with whispers and insinuations. They would divide, argue, and forget the purpose of the feast—namely me.

I could don a different appearance easily enough, though the thought of being in their midst wearing the face of another felt cowardly. Clearly, I wasn't going to enjoy the grand entrance I longed for, but I would attend as myself.

"Go on," I prompted Hulla, suspecting the clever woman had an answer to my problem.

"In this dress, with your hair and face hidden, they will think you are a servant. On feast days, they bring many extra serving women to court, so a new face will not raise suspicions. But," she hesitated and dropped her gaze.

"Say what you will, Hulla. I will not be angry."

"You must not act like a queen. If they call you for food or drink, you must serve the others and you must stay far away from Queen Ishtar and Lord Enki, for I believe they will know you despite your dress." Hulla bowed her head and waited.

"That makes perfect sense, Hulla. You are wise, and I will not forget your kindness today." I straightened my shoulders as my excitement mounted. I could play a servant for the day if it meant being among the living. If no one knew I stood among them, their homage would come from their hearts and not because my presence pressured them. It would make my celebration even sweeter.

I lifted my veil and kissed Hulla's cheek, understanding how she had snared Namtar's attention. "Thank you again, Hulla. You will have many blessings when you reach my hall in Irkalla, though I hope I do not see you for a very long time."

Hulla bowed and ushered me out. Namtar nodded his approval as I emerged from the hut. He lingered to speak quietly to Hulla as I wandered a little way up the path that led to the town. The stream of shades and spirits trudged on, mostly unseeing or uncaring about the world around them. They followed the insistent call to the Underworld. They would await my judgement and spend the rest of eternity in the dark. They gave me a wide berth, some of them looking at me curiously, feeling my power but unsure at who or what I was.

As Namtar joined me, a man, mortal and very much alive, hurried past. He bowed to Namtar but brushed by me like I was as invisible as the spirits that walked beside him. I whirled around to address the man, whose robes swirled and billowed in his haste. Hulla caught my eye and shook her head, reminding me of my role. I swallowed my rebuke and Namtar gave Hulla a quick wave before turning to stride away down the road, leaving me to scramble to catch up.

We joined the mass of people walking along the road toward the city. Namtar strode confidently forward, without a backward glance. I hurried to keep pace, staying a few feet behind him as he wound his way around slower travelers. The dust rose around us as we jostled along, rubbing shoulders with dozens of others. I caught snippets of their conversations as they talked about the prices at the market and the heavenly feast. I wanted to linger and listen, but Namtar kept a demanding pace. Finally, the road widened as we neared the city walls and the congestion thinned. Namtar slowed his speed and waited for me to fall into step beside him.

"Hulla told me of your plan to disguise yourself as a servant. So far, I'm impressed, but this is just the start, mother. Hulla warned you what will happen if they discover your deception." Namtar spoke softly, though I didn't know why he bothered. No one paid us the least attention. They were all consumed by their business, thoughts, and worries as we marched along the dusty road.

"Hulla is an exceptional woman." I watched Namtar's face. The flare of pride and affection in his eyes warmed my heart. My son was in love, something I never considered possible for a soulless child of the Land Between.

Perhaps on this day, when the Queen of the Dead walked among the living, anything was possible.

CHAPTER SIX

As we drew closer to the gates of the city, traffic slowed to a crawl and Namtar explained the rise of the city, Eridu, over the centuries. Home to many temples and a center of commerce and wealth, many called it the City of the Gods, though the gods no longer dwelled there.

"The port is full of boats from upriver, as well as from the vast waters beyond the mouth of the Euphrates. The island kingdom of Dilmun trades dates, copper, and precious stones for wheat and barley grown outside the city. Enki and Anu both have enormous temples here," Namtar prattled on about the wealth and prosperity of the city, though I could see it written on the high rooftops of the multistory buildings that loomed above the city wall.

I hid my surprise that the gods had forsaken from their earthy homes. When I last walked in the light, mortals and gods lived together on the land while only Anu dwelled above. The mortals served the gods, and the gods educated and cared for the mortals. This vast city had been a village that clustered around a small reed-filled port.

Uncertainty and worry crept in as we walked. In the darkness for so long, I had no idea of modern customs. I knew nothing of these people's daily lives, judging the worth of their souls based on the purity of their heart. I cared nothing for how they lived day to day and paid little heed to them after I passed my judgement. They became one more shadow among countless others.

We filed through the city gates, and I pushed my doubts aside. Throngs of people moved in all directions. A cacophony of music and voices filled the air, along with the pungent odor of bodies, animals, and open sewers. I wrinkled my nose in distaste.

A market sprawled through the town. A wide avenue bisected it with narrow crossroads branching off at irregular intervals. Merchants' tents crowded either side of the road. Colors painted everything. Most of the merchants wore turbans and robes of bright red and yellow to boast their wealth. The stalls held everything from dates to silk to woven baskets. I tried to look everywhere at once and kept running into Namtar's back as he stopped and started along the congested path.

A large crowd of people clustered around a tent serving spiced beer and clouds of smoke billowed out of the hole in the ceiling. More people crowded to get in line, pushing in from all sides. I clutched Namtar's elbow as people pressed in. Sweat prickled on my skin as my heart hammered. People shouted their orders and shoved me to the side in their bid to make themselves heard. I stumbled and lost my grip on Namtar. A man stepped on my foot, and I pushed him away, anger rising in my chest. He didn't bother to apologize as he lowered his shoulder and wedged his way forward in the undulating sea of people. Another shove to my back sent me staggering into the massive chest of a man who had received his cup of beer. He spilled it down the front of his robes and glowered at me with murderous intent.

"You stupid cow." He roared in my face and drew his hand back to strike me.

The power of the earth, once something that hummed through me with every beat of my heart, rose to my call, eager and fresh. I caught the man's wrist and squeezed. He bared his yellowed teeth with a growl, like a feral animal. The stench of his breath made my stomach roll. People stepped away, giving us space. I tightened my grip until his growl faltered into a whimper.

"Kneel, dog." I commanded through clenched teeth. Waves of power thrummed through me, and I shook with the effort of keeping them in check.

He sneered at me through his pain but didn't comply; so, I broke his wrist with a satisfying crunch. He collapsed to his knees with a scream. People stared, and a hush fell over the crowd. Namtar fought his way through the crowd. He kicked the man on the ground, who curled around his broken arm with dust sticking to the tear tracks on his face.

"That's what you get for trying to steal from me. All of you mind your business!" Namtar yelled to distract the crowd before snagging my arm and dragging me away to a narrow side street. Behind us, the call for beer once again erupted. I glanced over my shoulder to see two men help their fallen companion out of the dirt.

Namtar hustled along, not letting go of my elbow as he wound through the city side streets. I wondered how he knew the city so well, since to my knowledge, he had only been here a handful of times. Maybe he was going further than Hulla's hut on his visits to the first gate. My son had secrets, and it pleased me his life held more than the shadows of death.

He kept his furious pace until we stood at the edge of the temple. I smiled at the stone façade that bore Anu's symbol. I knew this place, though it had grown from the single room mud brick structure I had last seen. Namtar guided us to a secluded corner just outside the entrance to the altar room. The cool shadows welcomed me, and my father's comforting warmth embraced me. I sighed with bliss, but Namtar whirled around, frowning at me with his brows drawn together in disapproval.

"You must remember your role. You are not a queen. You are a servant, and you should walk behind me. You will keep your eyes down. You will not speak unless spoken to. Do you understand, mother? You are not a queen today." He gripped my shoulders and gave me a little shake.

"That man was going to strike me. He should be dead for his insolence." Heady power coursed through me as I stood in my father's temple. The innate power of the gods flowed so easily here.

Namtar shook his head and closed his eyes for a moment, as if searching for patience. He opened his eyes and met my gaze with earnest intensity.

"When we arrive at court, do not follow me through the main entrance. Go around to the side where the serving women gather. Join them and find your way to the main hall. Just follow the flow and accept whatever job you're assigned. When you get to the great hall, stick to the edge of the room. Maybe no one will notice you, but if someone calls on you to serve them, you must do it without hesitation—even if it is Ishtar. Are you sure about this?" Namtar's words tumbled out as his gaze bored into me, trying to read my resolve.

I dropped my eyes and bowed my head. "Of course, my lord. Lead the way."

Namtar sighed and looked heavenward for a moment. Then he gave a short laugh. "That son of a goat collapsed like a tent without a pole." He shook his head and gave my shoulders a brief squeeze. "Have fun, Mother. You deserve it." He turned and entered the antechamber, and I fell in behind him like a dutiful servant.

I followed Namtar past the altar where the priests made their offerings and prayed in the shadows. We paused, kneeling at the altar to add our praises to the priests' chants. A steady stream of people did the same and we could not linger, though I would have liked to stay and listen to the rhythm of the prayers. I kept close to Namtar as we left the altar and exited the rear of the temple. Instead of spilling back onto the streets of Eridu, we mounted a staircase and ascended to the heavens.

The stairs rose before us, disappearing into the clouds. Several others attending the feast climbed with us, steadily marching upward. I observed the differences in their dress and bearing. Servants walked with a bowed head as their masters strode forward confidently. The intricately woven cloth of their robes dripped with brightly colored fringes and marked their status and wealth. The servants wore drab colors, much like my brown scarf and dress.

I glanced at Namtar, who walked through the crowd without giving them a second glance. Like everything in Irkalla, his garments faded to gray and brown when he was below. Here they shone with bright blue with green decorations. Even his hair reflected hues of subtle reds and browns. People stepped aside to let him pass, instinctively understanding his status, even if they did not recognize the Prince of the Damned.

Pride swelled in my chest as we wove through the crowd, climbing ever upward. I silently thanked the Father of All for sending him to me. If I had to play servant to anyone, I would gladly serve my son, for he deserved my loyalty. If not for him, I would have long ago withered to a shade among shades lost in the shadows of the Underworld.

Our arrival at the gate curtailed my musings, and I refocused my mind on the present. Despite Namtar's instructions, I lingered to steal a quick peek through the heavenly gates. I glimpsed a massive room with chairs and tables clustered together. Glittering white stone lined the walls and floor, and everything beamed with light. Giant trees with dark green waxy leaves hung over the room, creating a lush canopy that shaded the edges of the space. Flowers flowed in cascades of color in gardens, and fountains burbled with clear, cool water while a chorus of birdsong filled the air.

A sharp nudge from behind cut my ogling short.

"Put your eyes back in your head and get a move on, girl. You'll see it all soon enough. Though if you stand around gawking, you won't see it for long," a woman growled at me, steering me away from the splendor that beckoned me with a hard yank on my arm.

I gritted my teeth, biting back my retort, and kept my gaze lowered as I fell into step with the burly woman.

"First time to court, I imagine," she said, sounding like she had swallowed a bunch of rocks. Her round face bore deep lines around her mouth and across her forehead, and her jowls wobbled as she stomped along. She adjusted her head scarf, tucking a wayward lock of gray hair beneath the rough brown cloth, and looked at me from the corner of her eye. "Why the veil? Are you ugly?"

Her bluntness caught me off guard, and I drew myself

up before I thought better of it. "If they required a veil for ugliness, I believe you would wear one as well."

The woman's mouth split into a wide smile that revealed uneven yellow teeth, and she laughed as we joined the queue filing into a small alcove. "Indeed, child. I might not be pretty, but I know my place." Her tone grew serious. "You best learn yours, or it will be a short day for you."

I held my silence and gave her a curt nod. We followed the stream of serving women. We were each given something to carry into the great hall as we filed past the kitchens. When we got to the front of the line, the older woman took an enormous platter piled high with fruit and lifted it on her shoulder like it weighed nothing. I grabbed a pitcher of wine and hurried behind her. A short walk brought us to the great hall.

I hesitated at the threshold. My heart hammered in my chest as I took in the sun-drenched room. Everything sparkled with light and brilliance. The beauty stole my breath and tears filled my eyes. Once I passed my days here in innocence, coming and going as I pleased. I had long ago forced myself to stop dreaming of my days in the sun, but it all came rushing back.

I stood gawking, wanting to drink it all in, but a sharp word from the women behind me goaded me forward. I stepped into the heavenly court for the first time in centuries, clutching a wine pitcher to my chest and staring around with the wide eyes of a child.

Of course, my entrance went unnoticed. I pushed away the pang of disappointment, impatient with my runaway emotions. A small part of me had hoped someone would turn and point, recognizing me despite my disguise. They would cry, "The Queen of the Underworld is among us!" Joyous praises would fill the air as the court fell to their knees. I cut my daydream short and remembered Namtar's instructions.

Skirting the edge of the room, I found an out of the way spot beside the trunk of a large tree. Gods and goddesses sat talking. Mortals of high regard stood in small groups, chatting quietly. Servants roamed through the room, offering trays of food and refilling mugs. None of them seemed to notice the splendor that surrounded them.

A deserted stone bench sat beneath the tree, and I tucked my jug of wine behind the trunk and climbed up on the bench to see over the crowd. I smiled when I saw Enki talking with a man. His hands moved as he spoke, and I knew he must be describing how to build something. He drew a figure in the air, growing even more animated, and the man nodded. Enki loved nothing more than teaching and building. Some things never changed.

Ishtar lounged in a corner with our brother, Shamash, the Sun God. My fingers closed into tight fists as my hatred for her burned bright. I consoled myself that her beloved Dumuzid lurked in the shadows of my hall. Even the mighty Ishtar could not escape the laws of the universe, though I doubted losing Dumuzid pricked her stone heart.

I searched for Namtar and held my breath as the herald led him into the room.

"Lord Namtar, Emissary of Queen Ereshkigal!"

The pronouncement carried over the babble of conversation. The hall fell silent. Even the birdsong ceased as every creature turned to watch Namtar stride into the hall.

Time suspended for a heartbeat. I waited with my heart slamming hard in my chest. I imagined myself standing beside Namtar with my chin held high.

"I stand here in place of my mother, the Queen of the Dead, the Holder of Judgements, and Mistress of Darkness." Namtar swept the room with a level gaze, hesitating a fraction of a second on me, before turning to Anu, who rose from his seat at the high table.

"Namtar, we welcome you and offer blessings to my daughter, Queen of the Night, Mother of the Dead, Mistress of Irkalla and the Land Below."

I gasped in surprise as Anu, the Father of All, bowed his head to Namtar. Tears pricked my eyes as I saw my father pay homage to me and my realm. His godly radiance warmed the room and the rest of the gods quickly followed suit, dropping to their knees and lifting their voices in a shower of praise and blessings.

I felt a tug on my robes. The old woman from the stairs gestured for me to kneel. I hopped off the bench and dropped to my knees next to her, though I didn't press my head to the floor as she did. I watched with satisfaction as Ishtar lowered herself with Shamash beside her, murmuring their well wishes.

The wave of kneeling and blessings swept through the hall until it stuttered to a stop as a lanky god folded his arms across his chest and leaned defiantly against the white stone wall. The moment swelled, silent and tense. Namtar's eyes narrowed in anger at the god's disrespect, but before he could issue a challenge, Enki leapt to his feet, calling for the feast to begin. A general sigh of relief rippled through the assembly as they found their seats according to their station and waited with anticipation for the first course.

I stood, picking up my jug of wine. Rage beat in my breast. How dare he not bow? How dare he show such blatant disrespect for my sovereignty over life? He would learn how to bow in proper deference to the Queen of the Damned. I edged around the room, following the god as he sauntered toward the high table, seeking a seat for the feast.

"Wine!" Namtar's voice called over the general thrum of conversation.

I cut between tables as I closed in on my objective. He must pay his respects like every other god and creature had.

"Wine!" Namtar bellowed again.

The burly old woman stepped in front of me, barring my path. She set her hands on her hips. "Pay attention," she snapped. "Lord Namtar wants your wine, you fool."

I stared at her, ready to strike her down before I moved on to deal with the insolent god. Fury flamed in my soul. I would show him the power of death. I would suck the life force from him until he cowered at my feet. My heartbeat pounded in my ears, feeding my rage.

"I would like some wine," Namtar said from behind me, interrupting my rampaging thoughts.

I whirled around, sloshing wine over the edge of the jug. Dark purple liquid splashed on the hem of Namtar's robes. The old woman huffed in irritation behind me and elbowed me out of the way, taking the jug and filling Namtar's mug.

"I'm sorry, Lord Namtar," the gravelly voice rasped. The woman bowed low over the jug, backing up. She grabbed my hand and jerked me down into a bow beside her.

Namtar waved her apology away. "Court can be overwhelming if you're not used to it," he said, sending me a warning look before he turned away to take his seat of honor at Anu's left hand.

The old woman thrust the jug back in my hands. "That's your last chance. You'll be out on your ear if it happens again."

I restrained myself from upending the jug over her head and filled the cup that someone thrust in front of me. I moved through the tables, filling cups until the jug was empty, and then escaped to the back corner of the room, abandoning the jug and the pretense of serving. I tucked myself into the shadows and pulled them tightly around me. I breathed a sigh of relief as I hid from view and settled in to watch with mounting anticipation of the honors that were yet to come.

CHAPTER SEVEN

*E*nki made the first toast.
"Blessings to my little sister, whose beauty and innocence I miss terribly. May her wisdom and grace never falter."

Every cup, even the insolent god, raised in unison to echo Enki's well wishes. Next, Shamash stood and, in his radiance, blessed my darkness and sacrifice as the ruler of the dead. A small army of serving women entered hauling trays heaped with roast goat. The crowd tucked in eagerly.

The assembly talked and laughed as they ate and drank. I listened to the snippets of conversation. They talked of ordinary things. Many worried about the state of the crops and the health of their animals. The gods complained about the condition of their temples and the decline in the number of offerings. The mortals grumbled among themselves about the petty selfishness of their overlords.

The sparkle dimmed on the heavenly court as the day wore on. Courses came and went. With each one, someone raised a toast to my health that Namtar graciously accepted. He looked bored as he raised his mug for the seventh time but answered Anu with a clever story when he asked about his messenger, Belanum.

"The stairs from Irkalla are twice as many as to the heavens. He was tired when we emerged from the Underworld. I sent him to rest, assuring him I could see myself the rest of the way," Namtar explained, and Anu nodded, moving on to speak to Shamash.

Enki, however, narrowed his eyes and scanned the room. I shrank deeper into the shadows, hoping he wouldn't pursue the matter. Ishtar stood, distracting him, and commanded the room's attention as she told a story about establishing the natural order on earth. It was an old tale, but everyone fell under her spell as she recounted the disputations that shaped our world. No one noticed when I slipped out of the room.

I couldn't stay a moment longer. I didn't belong to this glittering world. I couldn't stomach that banal chattering and whining. I ruled a kingdom of darkness where dangers lurked, and judgements weighed heavily in the shadows. I sat on a throne with a legion of souls and spirits at my feet and while it drew out into a monotonous existence, at least it had a purpose. The trivial nonsense of this court baffled me.

When had the gods become detached from the world? What gave them the right to demand offerings from the mortals when they gave nothing in return? Figureheads, empty of purpose, sat around those tables. Disgusted and disappointed, I wandered into an empty courtyard outside of the hall. This day in the light had not turned out the way I envisioned.

I sighed as I sat on the edge of a fountain and stared into the heavens. The stars winked and danced above and dulled my irritation. I searched for the Great Bull and smiled when

I saw his stars shining brightly. It was a good place for the sweet Gugalanna. A quiet peace filled me, soothing the wound in my soul. He would stand proud and watchful for eternity. If nothing else, seeing him among the stars made this trip worthwhile.

"It's terrible, isn't it?"

I jumped and looked over my shoulder. My eyes widened as the insolent god strolled into the small courtyard. I stood, crossing my arms over my chest, and glaring at him through my veil.

"I imagine nothing is to your liking. Only someone with immense arrogance could find fault with the stars' perfection." I kept my anger on a tight rein as I reminded myself that I could not reveal my identity. I dearly wanted to throw off my veil and let death look him in the eye. A smile tugged at my lips as I imagined him quivering at my feet.

He raked a hand through his black hair, brushing it off his forehead and looked up at the night sky.

"Oh, I have nothing against the stars. They're pretty enough, though I have seen things far prettier here on earth." He walked past me, close enough his shoulder brushed mine. "I meant this feast for a queen who can't even attend. These things are painful enough to endure, but now Anu is putting them on for anyone he feels sorry for."

I spun around to face him, but he stared up at the stars with his hands clasped behind his back. I took a deep breath and made sure I had my temper firmly in check before responding.

"Why would Anu feel sorry for the Queen of Irkalla? She rules a powerful kingdom that even the heavenly court fears. He celebrates her as he should, though I noticed you did not bow."

I studied his face as he continued to gaze into the

heavens with no sign of hearing my words. With no beard to soften the hard angles of his face, he bore an intense appearance even as he did nothing more than look at the sky. He carried a ferocity that simmered just beneath his skin, like a creature ready to strike.

"Why would I bow to a queen I do not fear? Death holds no power over a warrior, for she is a constant companion on the battlefield. She chooses the warriors worthy of continued life and grants a glorious death for those who are not." He spoke softly, his voice smooth and low, and glanced at me.

"Should you not bow to show your respect for the one who decides if you live or die? Would you not want to win her favor?" I asked, intrigued despite my irritation.

"I'm the greatest warrior ever to walk this land. Lady Death cannot reach me. I bow only to those who deserve it."

His power drew me to him, like a bee to sweet nectar. Everything about him radiated arrogance, selfishness, and unshakeable confidence. I wanted to rise and crush him under the weight of death. I wanted to teach him humility and to respect the ultimate power of the universe. But just as badly, I wanted to taste him, to drink in his ferocity. I wanted this man to worship me. Lust and longing raced through me. Different from what Kur had stirred earlier, this attraction demanded action, demanded release.

Rage and hunger boiled within me, bringing the visage of death to the surface. I turned away from him as I wrestled with my emotions. He spoke like he knew the Queen of the Dead, though we had never met. This god had not walked the earth during my time in the light, but I believed him to be the God of War.

Born in the bloodlust of that first war that exiled me to the darkness, the God of War stirred the hearts of man with a fever to conquer and kill. During times of war, the battlefield became an extension of Irkalla. In those dark times, I roamed through the battle, wrapped in the shadow of death, granting life or death to the warriors.

This arrogant god thought he was beyond my grasp. I would teach him otherwise. I would inspire the respect he lacked. Another wave of heady power rolled through me at the thought, but even as temptation beckoned, I knew this was not the time for such a lesson. I took a deep breath, pushing away the desire to reveal myself and instruct him on the power of death.

Once again in firm control of my emotions, I turned back to face him and found him blatantly studying me. His gaze roamed over me with the same intensity he had shown the stars. I thanked the heavens for the thin barrier of the veil. His green eyes reflected intelligence, strength, and more arrogance than any one being should have.

He stepped toward me, reaching for my veil. "Who are you? A servant who has the bearing of a goddess and stands here challenging me. I feel your power, but I do not know you." He murmured the words in a silky whisper that made me shiver.

My heart hammered and though I knew I should turn away, he snared me with his jade eyes boring into mine. I licked my lips as heat unfurled within me. The blazing flames of hunger, lust, and desire roared to life. My breath hitched and a soft moan escaped me before I pressed my lips together. His eyes flared with interest and excitement as his fingers touched my face through the veil, tracing them downward to the edge of the cloth. I held my breath as another tremor ran through me.

"My Lord Nergal, God of War, Destruction, and Pestilence! You and I need to talk." Namtar's voice cut through the suspended moment. Anger sharpened his words, and reality viciously reinstated itself.

Father Above, what am I doing? I whirled away from Nergal's hand and ran. Namtar addressed the God of War, but I couldn't make out the words. I ran headlong down the heavenly staircase and through Anu's temple, ignoring the startled gasps from the priests as I didn't offer thanks at the altar. As I shoved and pushed my way through the crowds of Eridu's market, curses chased me through the city gate. The traffic on the road had lightened, and I ran without stopping all the way to Hulla's small mud hut at the entrance to Irkalla.

Hulla greeted me with a surprised look but invited me in and offered me refreshment.

"No, Hulla. Thank you. I will wait here for Namtar," I announced and pulled off the veil, dropping onto a reed chair and pulling in a shaky breath.

Hulla gasped and concern clouded her face. "What happened, my queen?"

I frowned at her. "What do you mean? Nothing happened," I snapped. "It was a dreadfully boring, stupid feast, and I'm glad I don't have to attend them."

Hulla's brown eyes widened, and she looked uncertain. I softened my tone.

"Forgive me, Hulla. It was a long day, but why do you ask?" She looked at me like I had sprouted two heads.

"It's just your eyes. They're full of flames."

CHAPTER EIGHT

I slumped in the chair and sipped the cup of wine Hulla pressed in my hand as my heart slowed from its hammering gallop. The inferno blazing within me cooled to embers, and I knew my eyes no longer danced with flames when Hulla held my gaze with a tentative smile. We sat in a terse silence that I couldn't summon the energy to break. Relief smoothed the worried lines from Hulla's brow when Namtar swept through the door.

"Mother Goddess and all her goodness, what were you doing?" He demanded, kneeling in front of me, concern and anger alternating in his expression.

I frowned, aggravated at his chastisement, but I reminded myself that I deserved it. I hadn't stuck to the plan and nearly revealed myself. I swallowed my scathing rebuff and focused on controlling my emotions lest I unleash the fire within me again.

"I'm sorry, Namtar. I got carried away. The God of War, Nergal, did not bow." My tone turned frosty as I remembered his insolence.

Namtar nodded, his expression tight with irritation. "I spoke with him about that, and Enki assures me he will deal with Nergal."

I raised my eyebrows. I doubted Enki's idea of dealing with the situation would be anything like mine.

"Exactly what did my brother suggest would be a fitting punishment for that stiff-necked, arrogant power monger?" I didn't mention his intoxicating green eyes or the way his power drew me like a thirst that only he could quench. No matter how he made me feel, he insulted me in front of the entire court. That could not go unanswered.

Namtar looked uncomfortable and shifted his gaze to look out the window.

I barked a short laugh. "Let me guess. Enki will counsel him on proper etiquette. The God of Wisdom always seeks to educate, but he cannot teach humility. That is learned through pain and submission." The embers within me stirred, and the flames once again rose.

Hulla gasped and covered her mouth with her hand. She stepped closer to Namtar, who put a arm around her shoulders.

"Mother, we are in Hulla's home. You will not frighten her." Namtar's sharp words punctured the growing storm, and I drew my hand over my face, rubbing my eyes.

"Apologies, Hulla," I said with genuine contrition. I had no desire to terrify the woman who had shown me every kindness. "As I said before, it has been a long day. I believe it is time to return below. Hulla, could you take a message to Lord Enki?"

"I will take whatever message you have to send, Mother. Leave Hulla out of this."

Hulla and I frowned at Namtar in unison. She straightened and shook off Namtar's supporting arm.

"I am happy to serve you in whatever small way I am able," Hulla replied with a small bow.

I smiled, admiring her strength. "This message must come from one who has no ties to me. Therefore, there can be no question that the words come from my lips and mine alone." I explained the importance of an impartial messenger to forestall Namtar's objections. "Hulla, tell Lord Enki, I have heard of the disrespect shown in the heavenly court, and my anger blazes hot. The strength and might of the Underworld are beyond question. I will release all the darkness of Irkalla if Nergal, God of War, does not present himself before me on bended knee." I pulled out a silver strand of my hair and handed it to Hulla. "You'll give that to Lord Enki to verify your message. Tell him of my displeasure and sincerity. I will not allow an insult like this to go unanswered."

Hulla paled under my declaration, but she nodded again. "I will tell him, my queen," she whispered and wove the strand of hair around her fingers.

I stood and addressed Namtar. "You will wait here for Hulla to return with news from Enki. I have souls to judge and a kingdom to rule and have no time to waste on a minor god in need of an attitude adjustment. Be well, my son, and Hulla," I waited for the woman to look at me and felt a pang of remorse for the fear I saw on her lovely face, "You have my blessings and my admiration."

Wonder replaced some of the terror in Hulla's kind brown eyes. She bowed and Namtar opened the door for us. She headed toward the road and Eridu as I hurried to the gates of my kingdom, eager for the shadows to cool my fevered skin.

Neti bowed low as he opened the gate and accompanied me as we descended the stairs. We walked in silence, but I could feel him bursting with questions. As we reached the doors of Ganzir, I paused and looked at my loyal gatekeeper.

"We will have a visitor soon and must be on guard for tricks. He doubts the strength of this realm. He will not leave until he acknowledges it." I spoke the words through mounting excitement, stirred more from seeing Nergal again than indignation at his insolence.

Neti nodded. "I will reinforce the gates and increase the guards."

"Do not interfere when he arrives. He is to be shown every honor as a guest and ushered straight to me. However, he must not leave until I release him."

"I understand, my queen," Neti replied and bowed low.

Jaz burst through the doors of the palace and glowered at me in my brown robes that were rapidly fading to gray. Neti mumbled an excuse to scamper back up the stairs to his post. I pulled the scarf and veil off my head and unwove Hulla's beautiful handiwork, shaking down my hair. Jaz crossed her arms over her chest, watching me with a furious frown.

"So, you went through with your madness? How did you find the heavenly court? I heard there was trouble."

I smiled at her, wanting to make peace and unsurprised that her network of shadows and demons had brought the story ahead of me.

"It was dreadful. There wasn't a demon to be seen." I winked as I pushed past her into the palace, and she followed as I made my way to my rooms.

Once there, I told her the story. She looked smug when I described the sun burning my skin but outraged when I explained how Nergal had refused to bend his knee. When

I told her about our encounter in the courtyard, I glossed over the attraction I felt and focused on his arrogance and opinion of death.

Jaz's expression clouded with fury and indignation. "We must deal with this. Of all the gods, the God of War should show respect to the power of death. Shall I go to him, slip in next to him while he sleeps, and wrap him in the warm embrace of Irkalla?" Her eyes flashed red as she smiled, warming to the idea. "The exquisite torture I would give him until he begged for your forgiveness makes my blood sing."

A flash of irrational jealousy shot through me at the idea of Jaz touching him. "No," I said far too strongly and hurried to add, "He will come to me." I filled her in on the last part of the story. "And once he bows to his queen, he will stay forever." The memory of the fire he lit was already fading, sucked beneath the draining cold of the Underworld. "Be sure to send Belanum on his way. Anu asked about him. He is still alive?"

Jaz rolled her eyes. "I'll see him on his way. His whimpering is tedious, and he hasn't stopped complaining about the cold."

"Just make sure he sees the other side of the gate in one piece." Jaz turned to leave. "Could you send in a bath?" I called after her.

Jaz nodded without breaking stride and left me to stare into the fire until a crew of demons pushed through the door with steaming buckets of water. They filled the stone tub in the corner of the room and left as silently as they had come. I sighed as I slipped into the steaming water. My skin should burn and flare red, but only the slightest touch of warmth penetrated. Disappointed, I closed my eyes.

I searched for the heat, the roll of excitement in my belly, any sensation that reminded me of what I felt when Nergal touched my face. His jade green eyes came to mind with a flutter of butterfly wings in my chest. I focused on it, tried to hold on to the sparkle of the stars and the heat in his gaze, but the great void of Irkalla stripped the memory of all its colors. I bit my lip as it faded to black and white. A pang of grief gripped my heart. I could not stand an eternity of this numbness.

"Did you have a good time at your celebration?" A voice like stone on stone broke through my misery.

I didn't open my eyes. "Go away, Kur. You're not welcome here." I knew my words would go unheeded, but I said them anyway. I didn't want him here, witnessing my return to the monotone existence he sentenced me to.

Kur echoed my sigh in mock empathy. "Poor queen, brought back to a kingdom she never wanted."

I opened my eyes a crack and looked at him. In his human form, his midnight skin reflected the firelight as he sat on the edge of the tub, facing me. His loin skirt rode up, exposing a muscular thigh as he stared down at me with his golden gaze. I sank lower in the tub until the water met my chin. His teeth flashed white as he smiled.

"I know what you need."

His words rumbled low in his chest as he dipped his hand into the water. I shifted away from it, sloshing water over the side. Kur laughed, a low rumble in his chest, and his golden eyes flashed.

I drew a breath to call Jaz, pulling my feet under me to launch out of the tub, when I felt the heat. I let the breath go with a sigh as the water wrapped me in a searing embrace. All my intentions melted away, and I relaxed back into the tub, letting my eyes drift closed.

"The God of War did not pay his respects." Kur's voice tugged me back from the pleasurable abyss that beckoned me. Of course, he had heard the whispers from the shadows.

"I have dealt with Nergal." Aggravated with myself for continuing the discussion, I drew a breath to dismiss him again, but he skimmed his fingertips over the tops of my breasts. I jerked in response, sloshing more water over the edge as a flash of desire undercut my irritation. My nipples drew tight, and I bit my lip to stifle a whimper of pleasure.

Kur pressed his advantage, exploiting my weakness. His tone softened. "He must learn the Underworld's strength. They all need to be reminded that the darkness holds the ultimate power. Why should we stay beneath their feet? Why should we cling to the shadows, unable to cross into the light as we please? Why must you disguise yourself to walk among your peers? You are a goddess and a queen." His fingers traced patterns over my shoulders and chest, dripping hot water down my skin.

Lulled by the heat, I let my thoughts drift. I imagined presiding over them, reveling in the image of Ishtar on her knees with her forehead pressed to the ground. Enki and Anu bowed humbly. The stiff-necked Nergal pressed my hand to his lips as he knelt before me. They sang praises in my name and begged for my mercy.

Could Kur be right? Did we need to rule the light and the shadows? I thought of the heavenly court and their banal chatter. Did I truly envy that? Maybe not, but how could I survive in the numbness of the dark? I reached for the flames that responded so readily just hours before, but the more I called to them, the further they receded. I ground my teeth in frustration and hated the tears that rose in my eyes.

"Relax," Kur murmured, drawing his fingers along my

neck to trace my jaw. "Beautiful, lonely queen. You don't need to do anything right now. Just think about it." Kur stirred the water again, infusing it with his radiating heat. It slid along my skin, surrounding me, and leaving me shivering as steam billowed from the surface of the water. A sigh of lust escaped as I forgot about everything except the erotic caress that gripped me.

I waited for my inner fire to roar in response to Kur's call. I wanted to feel it again, searing my heart and filling me with a pounding desire. Nothing happened. His embrace engulfed me, stroked me, aroused me, but nothing within me ignited. Nothing rose from the ashes of my soul and danced with power and promise.

Frustrated, I pushed to my feet, sending a cascade of water everywhere, and shoved Kur off his perch. As he steadied himself, I slung my robe around my shoulders and stepped out of the tub.

"Get out. I will have every demon, shade, and monster at my command hunt you until the end of days if you do not leave this instant." I ground the words out between clenched teeth and a flicker of power stirred as I set my feet in challenge.

Kur's golden eyes flashed, and a corner of his mouth turned up in a grin. "As you wish, my queen," he rumbled as he dissolved into the shadows.

I curled on the bed, pulling a thick blanket over me. Kur's words opened long harbored wounds of resentment. I hated him, but I couldn't deny the truth in his words. Over the centuries, the melancholy of my kingdom dulled my senses and eroded my will. I existed day after endless day fading into a pale shadow version of the goddess I once was.

Fatigue dragged my lids closed over my eyes. My tired

mind willingly gave up the fight for consciousness. I fell asleep with one thought standing out among the rest. I would not live as a shadow among shadows. Somehow, I would burn within the darkness.

CHAPTER NINE

"Get up." Jaz dropped my breastplate along with the rest of my armor at the foot of my bed.

I cracked my eyelids open. Jaz stood with her arms crossed over her chest, glowering at me. I scrubbed a hand over my face and sat up.

"What's all this?" I asked, gesturing to the pile of glittering bronze and hardened leather.

"We haven't sparred in ages. Last time we did, you could barely lift the sword. You've challenged the God of War and you must be ready to defend yourself and your kingdom. Now, get up." Jaz yanked the covers back and threw my battle garments at me.

I knew better than to argue or try to delay. Her foul temper radiated from her as she strapped my armor around me, cinching it with angry jerks and tugs. Finally, she turned and stomped out of the room, leaving me to jam my helmet on my head and follow in her wake.

In the training chamber, Jaz wasted no time. I had just entered the room when she spun, her short sword slicing through the air in a vicious arc. I dove out of the way, rolling back to my feet and pulling my sword from its scabbard.

"The God of War will not check his swing. He would be claiming the throne right now over your decapitated body."

I gritted my teeth. Jaz wouldn't hear excuses. I set my feet as she came at me once more. This time, my blade met her with a clang of metal. Relentless, she swung again and again. I parried each of her thrusts, and soon, my skin ran with sweat. We hammered each other with blow after angry blow. Finally, she sheathed her sword. I followed suit, simmering with aggravation at her heavy-handed tactics and remorse for the tension that hung between us.

"Enough. You have recovered some of your strength. Perhaps your insane trip to the heavenly court bore some fruit after all." Jaz untied my breastplate as she spoke. As she pulled my sword belt off, I caught her arm and held her until she stilled and faced me.

"I'm sorry I didn't heed your guidance, and I'm sorry I left you behind." I wasn't sure which was the bigger betrayal in her eyes.

Jaz's mouth tightened, and she nodded. "I exist to protect you. Without that, I am nothing." She whispered the words and dropped her gaze to study the sword in her hands.

I knew the words cost her dearly. They held power. By saying them, her vulnerability took shape for anyone who cared to exploit it.

"Look at me, Jazaroon, demon of dragon's blood and darkness, first among your kind, warrior, guardian, friend." I squeezed her arm when I said the last word and waited for her to lift her gaze to mine. "You are many things, but more than anything, you are my friend. I will do better at honoring that in the future."

Jaz held my gaze for a long moment before giving me a curt nod. It was quite the display of emotion for a demon. I smiled for both of us as she collected my armor and hung it in its place on the wall. She had crafted each piece in the early days of our kingdom, forging the suit for me in the deepest pits of the earth. Tempered with the magic of Irkalla and forged in dragon's fire, every piece fit me perfectly and would protect me from most magical and physical attacks. Of course, every armor had weaknesses and Jaz trained me to know mine. Until now, I never faced the real possibility of using it. The thought twisted my gut with unease, but I reminded myself that Jaz was preparing me for the worst case scenario, as was her duty. There was no need to worry about something that might not happen. If it did, Jaz and I would face it together.

I led the way from the training chamber. In my absence, the business of sorting souls had gone undone. Throngs of shades milled around the caverns, lost and uncertain. As I walked among them, they bowed and murmured their praises and pleas. I spoke to each one, raising them from their knees and peering into their eyes to judge their soul.

The warriors met the stare of death without flinching, proud to be received by the Queen of Irkalla. They would have a seat in my hall. Old women smiled as I raised them from their knees and their souls reflected contentment in a life well lived. They would find rest and ease—as much as one could in Irkalla. The children's purity shone in their eyes and their innocence lit even the impenetrable darkness of the Underworld. They, too, would join us in Ganzir.

Hiding in the shadows, I found the men who had not found honor in life, who did not worship their gods, who harmed their fellow man, who brutalized those who were weaker. These men cowered before me and when they met the stare of death, they withered to wraiths under the weight of their sins. Their screams echoed through the realm as the shadows claimed them.

When I finished my task, the realm settled as everyone fell into their places according to their rank and judgement. Quiet rustling, punctuated by the occasional whimper, set in as the host resumed its eternal vigil of the living and waited for something to happen. I turned back toward Ganzir but glanced up the grand staircase—again.

"Waiting for someone?" Jaz grumbled.

"Has Namtar returned?" I asked, though she and I both knew it wasn't Namtar that I was looking for.

"I have, Mother." Namtar's voice came from behind us, and I spun around to see him striding out of the great hall. A scowl twisted his handsome features. "I just left Hulla at her home in care of her mother. You should not have asked her to do that."

I raised an eyebrow at my son and felt a flicker of power in response to his challenge. I seized it, eager to recapture the spark. Like an ember in a fire grate, it needed gentle coaxing. Carefully, I fanned it with the aggravation at Namtar's audacity to question me. The spark heated, and I fed it my resolve to burn away the shadows that threatened to erase me.

"I would remind you, my son, that I am the queen of this realm. My decisions are not to be questioned. Hulla is strong and more than capable of the task I set her. She will suffer no lasting damage for carrying my message, and her rewards will be great."

Warmth spread through my belly and chest. For centuries I had walked these halls cold and hollow. Had this power been within my reach the entire time? Namtar's scowl deepened at my rebuke. All the power in the universe would mean nothing, if I lost the ones I held dear. I softened my tone.

"Tell me what happened."

I sat on the stone stairs that led into the main entrance to Ganzir and patted the space next to me, inviting Namtar to sit beside me. He continued to glower but dropped onto the stones next to me. Jaz took up her customary position behind my left shoulder with her arms crossed over her chest and demon eyes searching for threats. The surge of heat continued to burn like a gentle glow, and I relaxed, patting Namtar's knee. He gave me a sideways look. Never one to hold onto anger, his good humor restored itself and a slight grin tugged at his lips.

"I accompanied Hulla to the heavenly court." He held up his hand to forestall my reprimand. "I stayed hidden as she delivered your message. She was fierce as she marched into the court and demanded to be heard." His face shone with pride, and I glanced up at Jaz. She raised an eyebrow.

"She sounds like a warrior worthy of Irkalla," Jaz said.

"She's perfect," Namtar said and turned his face away for a moment to hide his blush.

I hid my smile and squeezed Namtar's knee. "Hulla is indeed a remarkable woman. However, we can sing her accolades another time. Tell me what happened when the court heard my message."

Namtar turned toward me and leaned forward. His grin widened, and his eyes danced with mirth and mischief.

"You should have seen them, Mother. The thought of Irkalla rising against them sent them into a frenzy. They wrung their hands and tore their hair, thinking about the armies of the dead swarming across the land. Most of them wanted to toss Nergal through the gates and lock them behind him. The God of War doesn't have many friends in the heavenly court."

I laughed at Namtar's description, and the warmth within me flared slightly. I straightened my shoulders, gazing over my kingdom that stretched further than I could see. They should be scared. Invincible and unafraid, the dead were the ultimate warriors. The insatiable darkness knew no fear and would consume everything in its path.

Namtar regarded me for a moment before he flicked a glance at Jaz, who said nothing but gave an infinitesimal nod.

"What is it, Namtar? What do you see when you look at me?" I asked, curious and annoyed that he continued to treat me like a fragile old woman.

"I see a queen full of fire and fury. I see the goddess who gave me life and rules with confidence. I see someone I thought was lost." Namtar's words were gentle, and he took my hand in his. His eyes held tenderness and joy. "You've been fading, Mother, and I didn't know how to stop it. But, you seem much more like your old self, like before...." He trailed off, but I knew what he meant to say. Before they killed the Great Bull and took from me the only source of light in my endless night.

The events of the previous day had distracted me from my grief, but looking at my son, a pang of loss for his father shot through me. Namtar missed him too. He took my hand in his and for a moment we stared into the vastness of Irkalla, lost in our thoughts.

Gugalanna always used to say that I could light up the Underworld with my smile. I always thought it was the other way around. My steadfast, sweet husband. He had never stirred the embers of my heart the way Nergal had with a few short words, but I sorely missed Gugalanna's simple comfort.

Shaking off my melancholy, I squeezed Namtar's hand and steered the conversation back to his story. "Tell me the rest. Since Nergal is not cowering at my feet, I assume the heavenly court decided against banishing him to Irkalla."

Namtar nodded. "Enki, of course, had a plan. He used the hair you gave Hulla to weave a chair made of reeds. He told Nergal that he must use the chair to enter the gates and present himself to you in the hall of Ganzir. The Lady Ishtar offered to accompany him since she has balanced her debt to the realm."

Anger, hot and vengeful, erupted from the well of hatred I nurtured especially for my sister. If she dared set a toe within my kingdom again, she would understand that balance was determined by the one who read the scales.

Namtar's grin faltered at the venom in my expression. He swallowed and hurried to reassure me. "Anu forbid her to come anywhere close to Irkalla. He had no patience for her and said she was the reason for the current problems. Enki intervened before she could argue and ran down a list of rules for Nergal. The usual—don't eat or drink anything, don't take any offerings, don't speak to the dead. All the things they think make a difference. Enki took Nergal off for a private discussion, so I didn't hear everything."

My sudden anger shifted to a nervous excitement. Nergal was coming. I pushed to my feet and smiled down at my son.

"You did well, Namtar. Was Hulla alright after her trip to court?" I asked with sincere concern. I had no wish for any harm to befall her.

Namtar's mouth tightened slightly, but he nodded. "She

was overwhelmed and exhausted but honored to be of service to you."

I heard the disapproval in his voice but ignored it. "She's a fine woman, a woman worthy of my son's affection."

Namtar's expression softened, and he smiled tenderly at the mention of his beloved. My heart, faded, gray, and atrophied as it was, soared with happiness as I witnessed the face of my son's love. I studied him intently for a moment, trying to fix the memory of him like this. Only the strongest love could survive the drain of Irkalla, and I hoped their connection could endure.

I looked out over my kingdom again before I turned and walked up the stairs into the great hall of Ganzir. The door swung open at my command and all eyes turned to me. The shades shifted, and the shadows whispered as they regarded me, feeling the newly discovered energy coursing through me.

I smiled at the host clustered around the enormous plain stone tables, eating, drinking, and watching eternity trickle by. Changes were coming to the realm. I would take back control of my destiny, starting with Nergal, the God of War. He would be the first to feel the wrath of Irkalla.

"My honored guests," I addressed the host and silence fell at my words. "We're going to have a visitor."

CHAPTER TEN

*E*xcitement swept through the realm. Even the most miserable shades, the ones who moaned in the dark with only their wretchedness to keep them company, crept closer to the great hall to glimpse the God of War. In their monotone existence, even hearing the rustle of his robes or the sound of his sandals against stone would be a precious diversion. Among the higher ranks, they squabbled over seats, keeping the demons busy breaking up fights and quelling arguments. The shadows shifted constantly, fed by the anticipation of something new.

I wrestled with my eagerness in the privacy of my chambers. I paced back and forth as Jaz stood stiffly just inside the door, watching me with increasing disapproval. I changed my robes for a third time.

"Is there a tint of blue in this one?" I asked her, smoothing it over my curves and examining myself in the polished silver mirror. "I think it definitely highlights my figure better."

"It is the same as the two before it and every other garment you possess." Jaz's patience ended. "You are the

Queen of Irkalla. You could wear a filthy rag and it would not diminish you. Why do you care what you are wearing?" She stepped into my path with her arms crossed over her chest and a fierce scowl on her face.

I shrugged and turned away. Jaz knew me far too well to lie. Better to say nothing and try to divert her attention.

"Once Nergal gets here, he cannot leave. You have demons posted to secure all the gates?" I asked with my back to her as I stared at my reflection.

Jaz stomped over and put herself between me and the mirror. "You are acting like Ishtar with her fine robes and gems. This isn't about bending the God of War to your will. You want him. You desire him." She studied my face, but I couldn't meet her eyes. "By the darkness, Ereshkigal, do you think you can keep him locked away here forever? Do you think he will fall at your feet and adore you? Do you think he will love you?"

Her words lanced through me, and I flinched. She gave voice to all my fears. Jaz didn't mean to be cruel, but it wasn't a demon's nature to say pretty words to spare someone's feelings. The burning passion, the flame in my belly, had slipped away, eroded by my doubts and fear. Try as I might, I couldn't conjure it and the loss of it triggered a cascade of anxiety that pushed it even further from my reach. I bit my lip and finally put into words what churned in my gut.

"What if he doesn't kneel?" I whispered, staring at my feet. Nothing mattered if he didn't acknowledge my rule. If he wouldn't bend, I would never see those green eyes or feel the heat of his touch.

"Pick your head up," Jaz barked.

I snapped my gaze to her, bristling at her tone. My belly stopped tying itself in knots and filled with hot conviction. I drew a breath, a reprimand on my lips, when Jaz's mouth curved into a savage smile.

"That's what you'll do if he doesn't kneel. Show him your strength. He will bend—or he will break." Jaz's eyes flashed red as her excitement rose at the thought of battling the God of War.

I smiled back at her and quickly braided my hair. "Will you double check the preparations? I want to be alone for a moment to gather my thoughts."

Jaz bowed and stepped around me.

"Jaz," I said, stopping her at the door. "Thank you."

The demon said nothing as she slipped out the door. I sighed and dropped into the chaise by the fire. It flickered and flared. I could feel the slightest warmth on my fingertips when I held them over the flames.

"You'll burn yourself," Kur's voice came from behind me.

I closed my eyes as a shiver ran down my back. In my dreams, he and Nergal had blurred and blended as they fulfilled all their promises of pleasure. Between them, they devastated me with erotic passions that I'd never experienced, never considered. The intensity of the dreams stayed with me, beckoning me to explore, to slide into temptation. My core clenched with desire, and his familiar heat enveloped me as he stood behind me, placing his hands lightly on my shoulders.

I swallowed hard, fighting the urge to lean back against him. I could not trust him. This monster thought only of his own reward. He sought power above all else. I could not lose my focus no matter what pleasures he offered. I possessed my own fire, my own heat. I did not need his.

"The flames are not the danger in this room," I said, failing to set the intended edge to my voice. Instead, I sounded breathless, desperate and Mother Goddess, help me, I was. His nearness brought the inferno of lust from my dreams raging to the surface. The heat of my desire twined with my burning hatred and conviction to keep him at arm's length. I wanted him as much as I loathed him.

Kur laughed, a low rumble, and rubbed his thumbs in slow, massaging circles at the base of my neck. "The God of War could be our ally. Have you thought of that?"

My stomach lurched, and my mind spun in a dozen different directions. Images from my dreams of him and Nergal, one claiming my breast and the other my mouth, flooded my mind. Viciously, I shut down my arousal. I was a queen defending her realm, not a slave to bodily desires. I redirected the roaring flames in my core, lurching to my feet and out of Kur's reach.

"This is none of your concern, Kur." I crossed my arms over my chest as a barrier between us. Free from his befuddling touch, my mind sharpened. "There is no our, no we. You and I have no connection. You are nothing but a thorn in my side."

Kur's white teeth flashed in a quick smile, and he laughed again as he sat down in the spot I vacated. I looked away from the way the firelight danced on his freshly oiled, ebony skin. In my dream, his skin seared mine as his body pressed against me. I tightened my arms around me, dousing those flames with icy resolve. He would not manipulate me.

"No connection? Your body responds to me in this form. I can smell the lust coursing through you. I hear your heart hammering in your denial of the desire that beats within you. I'd call that a connection." To my surprise, desire flared in his golden eyes as his gaze roamed over my body. He wanted my touch, wanted to taste my fire.

A heady sense of power flowed through me. This

dragon-man, my captor, my tormentor, wanted me. I knew this newest ploy of presenting himself in such a tempting package was only part of a greater scheme in his bid for power, but he was playing a dangerous game—one that two could play.

"Have you considered what I said when we last spoke? Will you continue to allow the ones who dwell in the light to have supremacy over this world?"

I didn't answer. Arousing dreams aside, I had thought much about what Kur had suggested. Nergal challenged Irkalla's might, and he would soon see the error of his ways. The dark realm accepted nothing but absolute respect. But the universe possessed a balance, a harmony that I would not sacrifice—unless I had to. If Nergal refused to bend his stiff neck, then the light would feel the wrath of the darkness. However, I was not yet ready to share my thoughts with Kur. His body may call to mine, but I could not allow myself to forget the dragon I loathed lay just below his appealing surface.

Interpreting my silence as agreement, he continued, his excitement mounting as he spoke. "This is a perfect opportunity. You can convince the God of War to join Irkalla. Use all your queenly charms and he will align his powers with ours. We can rule this world. We will walk the land, free from the shadows. They will know our might and flee in the face of our power." Avarice clouded Kur's brilliant gaze as his message reverberated in the room.

Far from motivating me to embrace his position, Kur's words stripped away any doubt from my mind. Always the master manipulator, he sought to use me for his own gains. He wanted to rule absolutely and thought he could do it through me.

I would no longer be manipulated by gods or creatures

who thought I was too weak to wield the true power of Irkalla. I drew in a breath, feeding the embers of power that burned like a black hole in my core. Echoes of words spoken by the God of Wisdom came back to me.

You have more power than you know and carry enough light to banish even the darkest night. You must embrace the darkness before you can wield it.

I didn't need Kur's hypnotic heat. I didn't need to hide from the darkness. The shadows held all the power, all the potential I could ever want. Fool that I was, I'd spent so long mourning my lost place among the heavenly court. I would never again yearn for a place amid that whining, sniping group. I knew my purpose in the darkness and I would not let Kur or anyone else tell me how to use it.

Kur watched me with lust and hunger etched on his face. I wondered if he yearned for me or the dominance he sought. As energy rolled through me, he tensed, leaning forward as if drawn toward me.

Sitting next to him, I traced a finger down his muscular chest. He shuddered under my touch and a low rumble of contentment rolled through him. His hands curled into tight fists as his golden gaze flared. Waves of heat rolled off him, engulfing me.

My heart pounded as my body flamed red hot, inside and out. Sweat beaded on my brow, and I licked my lips, holding tight to my courage. I had spoken the truth when I called him dangerous. I could not underestimate him. As creator of this realm, his power rivaled mine, and there was no denying the desire I felt for him—no matter how much I despised myself for it. I danced on the cliff's edge between passion and control.

I held Kur's gaze as I drew my nails up his inner thigh. His arousal throbbed, and he groaned as I swept his loincloth to the side. I closed a shaking hand around Kur's engorged staff and gasped, trying to snatch my hand away. His hand covered mine, holding me firmly around him as my flesh burned. Molten heat roared through him as his dragon demanded release. My mind skidded to a stop as I thought of this incredible searing heat inside me.

If I was dancing on the cliff's edge before, I was clinging by my fingertips over the abyss now. I pulled in a deep, shuddering breath and forced myself to focus on my goal. I was the queen. I was in control.

"Do you feel this power between us?" I asked, husky tones betraying my excitement. "I have thought about what you said. No one could stand before us if we united, harnessed this power. I could be the queen above and below with all things under my command." I tightened my grip on his rock-hard shaft. Kur blew out a hissing breath between his teeth.

"Yes, my queen." His eyes glowed, unfocused and desperate.

I moved my hand slowly up and down his cock and skimmed my lips over his before murmuring against his ear, "You will wait for my command and when I have the God of War firmly on our side, we will unleash the terrors of Irkalla and claim the world for our own."

Kur's groan of pleasure shook the room. Fire flashed around us as he claimed my mouth in a bruising kiss. His mouth ravaged mine as he pulled me to him. I pressed against him, throbbing with need. His incredible, searing heat surrounded me. I tipped my head back as his kisses trailed down my neck, leaving me trembling. He raised his head and smiled down at me. His hand guided mine to stroke him and I pulled in a shaking breath as I watched our joined hands pleasuring him.

"You want this, don't you, Ereshkigal," he growled as he stood. His hips rocked, thrusting into our grip. "Say the words and I will give you all you want and more."

By the darkness, I did want it. I wanted to taste it, take it inside me. I ached for it.

Kur released my hand and fisted my hair, tipping my head back. He traced my lips with the tip of his burning cock. I opened my mouth with a sigh of longing, losing my focus in a wave of desire that stole every thought, every intention.

"You will get nothing until you do as I say. Tell me you want it," he demanded, pulling away from my hungry mouth.

Something jarred within me, penetrating the hazy desire. I licked my lips as I struggled against the pull of his heat, of his promises. A queen did not beg, certainly not before a creature she despised. Ruthlessly, I refocused on my objective and channeled my disgust with myself into action.

With a surge of energy, I pushed Kur away, hammering him with a blow hard enough to send him stumbling backward. He fell back onto the chaise with his cock standing firm and proud. He grinned and stroked himself, but the grin slid from his lips as I rose to tower over him, tapping into the full power of my kingdom. My beauty slipped away, and the terrible visage of death loomed over him.

"Do you see what you made me, Kur? Do you see the queen of Irkalla?" He nodded, his expression wary, but not fearful. "Do you doubt my power?" I reached a skeletal hand out to grasp his still turgid cock. He tried to shift away, but I tightened my grip. "Do you doubt my power?" I whispered, leaning in to press my cold, decaying flesh against him. I smiled as he shook his head with wide eyes.

I gathered all the horrors of the realm, channeling their terrifying energy through me as I embraced the full scope of death. I shook with the effort of containing it and held Kur's golden gaze until he looked away. This world he created, full of misery and darkness, was mine to command, though until that moment, I had never truly seized the power.

"You will come when I call you. Until then, get out of my chambers and stay out of my sight." I hissed against his ear, surrounding him in the icy embrace of death.

Kur, creator of Irkalla and creature darkness and doom, bowed his head and trembled in my grip. I released him and stood naked before him with my beauty restored. Heat filled every fiber of my being as he shivered and his cockstand withered. I raised an eyebrow. He glared at me before shifting to his dragon form and disappearing into the shadows.

CHAPTER ELEVEN

The wait for Nergal challenged me. I paced the tunnels of Irkalla full of power and without fear. My encounter with Kur left me edgy, full of unfulfilled need and hunger for something to soothe the raging beast within me.

Impatience and anxiety accentuated every moment, stretching it out in frustrating slowness. Simple things, like sorting souls, took ages as my attention wandered to the gates. The line of souls jammed as I gazed into the infinite darkness that swallowed the stairs to the land of the living. I brought myself back to my task with an annoyed reproach, only to do it again moments later. I finally abandoned the pretense altogether and slipped into the shadows to wait.

The host fed on my restlessness until the entire kingdom filled with constant shifting and muttering. The souls who earned their rest found no ease. The blessed found no peace in my hall. The tormented lived an eternity of suffering in every second. The monsters and demons in the darkness roamed the vast warren of tunnels and caverns, quarreling over nothing. Moaning echoes filled the air, punctuated by terrified shrieks and wails full of such sorrow the host wept.

Pressure built as tensions rose. Squabbles erupted into brawls among the dead. Jaz and her demons suppressed fight after fight until Jaz planted herself in my path and forced me to stop.

"Enough," Jaz hissed. Her demon form in full control, she loomed over me. Her massive, leathery wings snapped out and caged me before I could change direction and walk away.

I spun toward her, fury rising. "Do not cross me, Jazaroon." The power of the realm eagerly answered my call.

Jaz bared her fangs at me and her eyes flashed red. "This must end. Irkalla will tear itself apart if you do not settle yourself." The words grated out in a growling hiss.

I heard the truth in her words, but my anxiety severed the tether to rational thought. As the time passed, my concern that Nergal would not present himself had exploded, goading me to this almost frenzied state. I couldn't settle to anything—not feeding the host or sorting souls. The God of War must bow to me. The thought consumed me. His green eyes loomed in my thoughts, triumphant and arrogant. They taunted my every moment. Nothing mattered beyond seeing him humbled at my feet.

"You go too far." I growled at Jaz. The face of death emerged, and I concentrated the infinite power through me, rising to meet my friend's blazing eyes. "Release me." My words filled the chamber.

"Make me." The demon whispered, lifting her chin in challenge.

Novice that I was at handling the infinite power of the realm, I fought to control it. For a terrifying moment, I lost my bearings. The power swamped me, washing away the boundary between it and the one who wielded it. I gasped in awe at the immensity of my potential, and joy lifted my heart as colors danced in my mind.

Jaz laughed as I grew beyond the boundary of her embrace. She launched into the air with a stroke of her powerful wings. I dissolved into the limitless entity of death with no form or bounds, and Jaz shrieked her approval. I spread throughout the kingdom, touching every inch of stone while I filled every crevice and wrapped every creature in my embrace. The host froze and for a heartbeat, the kingdom of Irkalla was silent.

Queen. I am the Queen. I remembered who I was in the shifting energy that coursed through me. I came back to myself, finding my form and slightly disappointed that I still wore a drab brown robe, and my hair was silvery white. Some things were beyond even my control.

A sigh rippled through the host. They shook themselves as if coming out of a long, deep sleep. I felt the breeze on my cheeks as they settled in contentment.

Jaz landed with a heavy thud next to me, shifting back into her human form. She bowed and I pulled in a surprised breath. When she straightened, she said, "My Queen. You've taken a step toward fulfilling that title."

I pressed my lips together, aggravated she minimized my accomplishment even while she made a show of bowing to me. Demons were exasperating creatures.

"I haven't taken a step toward anything. I am the queen, and the title is mine beyond question." I glared at Jaz, but her stony expression didn't change.

"A queen earns her title, every moment of every day. Always, someone waits to take that title from you. The one who you wait for will take it without remorse if you give him a chance. There is more to being a queen than wielding power and doing your duties." She shook her head, "You still have much to learn."

A furie's scream pierced the silence, cutting off my retort.

"Anu save us," Jaz murmured as we turned toward the sound.

The creature landed before us. A human-shaped form of dancing shadows shifted as the furie spoke in a hiss. "The God of War has come. Neti secures the gates, but demons conjured of the One Who Knows stand watch."

I frowned and Jaz cursed under her breath. Enki, the God of Wisdom and Knowledge, had created a set of galla, demons made of mud and intention, to accompany Nergal, but I could not imagine to what end.

"Jaz," I began, but she was already striding away, a step ahead of me as usual.

The furie bolted into the air, a solid ball of darkness, and zipped away into the tunnels. I turned and glanced up the staircase. Nothing yet, but I would not meet the God of War at the foot of the stairs like an excited dog. He would come to me.

With a flare of exhilaration and a flush of desire, I swept up the stair of Ganzir and into the great hall. The host's attention snapped to me, and they all bowed. I turned and slowly lowered myself onto my throne.

"Be easy, my friends. Your queen is here."

The souls shifted, finding their places according to their ranks. They waited with their eyes fixed on the doors. Namtar stood to my left with a fierce frown etched on his handsome face. He rested a hand on my shoulder and squeezed gently.

An echoing boom followed by another louder crash rattled the doors. Heavy footfalls approached, and the doors of the chamber swung open. Jaz, with her wings unfurled and talons on display, shouldered through the door. She bared her fangs, and the host shrunk back into the shadows. Tucking her wings back, she shifted to the side.

The God of War emerged from behind the demon. He walked forward with a confident stride and looked around the great hall with interest. He said nothing as Jaz stalked behind him, her displeasure palpable. Nergal didn't seem to notice. He marched straight up to the raised dais where I sat as the host rustled and shifted in the shadows, trying to see without being seen.

My stomach flipped in anticipation. I held my breath as he looked up at me. His smile widened as his gaze wandered over me, appreciating what he saw. His insolence knew no bounds.

"It's a shame they locked you away down here, though in the world above, you would be one of many beauties. Here you seem even more lovely." Nergal gave no indication of bowing. He stood at his ease and raked the hair off his brow.

Anger flared hot in my belly while my mouth went dry with nervous excitement. I hadn't expected him to come in on bended knee, but his arrogance infuriated me. I turned a frosty smile on the God of War.

Jaz crowded in behind Nergal—close enough for her breath to ruffle his hair.

"Bow," the demon hissed.

Nergal ignored her. "As much as I despise the heavenly courts, at least a god can relax there. I find Irkalla rather spartan for my tastes." He folded his arms and looked around at the stone tables and benches. No trees or fountains decorated the hall. No servants bustled about. Silence and shadows were the décor of the Underworld.

Namtar stepped forward. "You stand before Ereshkigal, Daughter of Anu, Goddess of Death, Queen of the Damned. You *will* bow." Namtar's blade rang as he drew it from its scabbard.

Nergal flicked a glance at Namtar before waving his hand in dismissal. "We've been through this. I bow to those who earn it. A title is not but a name. What have you done to earn my respect, Ereshkigal?"

The host sucked in a collective breath. Namtar launched himself off the dais as Jaz closed a massive taloned hand around Nergal's neck.

"Stand down," I barked and Namtar's blade froze a breath away from Nergal's chest. I rose from my throne, looking down on the God of War. He stood relaxed in the demon's grip, unconcerned with the tip of the sword hovering near his heart. "Both of you, step away from our guest."

Namtar lowered his weapon, but Jaz tightened her grip. "If you wish to feel the sun on your face ever again, you will bow." She tightened her fist to emphasize her words.

"Jazaroon, release him." I let my power flow through me with my words and Jaz stumbled backward under its impact. She caught herself and straightened, shooting a furious glare at me. I glowered back until she dropped her gaze. "Everyone, leave us." I commanded.

The souls and shades hurried to do my bidding, rushing out the doors without a backward glance. Namtar frowned and sheathed his sword.

"I would like to stay, Mother," he said with a small bow. "Your safety—"

"Is not in jeopardy." I cut across him, furious he would question me. "I will speak to Lord Nergal alone and will not repeat my request."

Namtar's eyes hardened in disapproval, but he said nothing further as he spun on his heel and marched out of the hall. Jaz loitered near the doors. I glared at her, and she glared back. The moment stretched on and Nergal looked over his shoulder at the demon.

"She's not very well trained."

Jaz growled low in her throat and took a step toward Nergal. I held up a hand, and she stopped, breathing hard, cold fury rolling off her.

"She is the finest guardian and most fearsome warrior in all creation. Her dedication serves her well and her discipline is the only reason you are still standing." I looked at Jaz and nodded. Reluctantly, she retreated to the doors and stepped outside.

"Any time you'd like a demonstration of my training, I'll be happy to show you, my lord." Her final words dripped acid and Nergal smiled as she closed the door.

"It might be dreary, but so far it's far more interesting than Anu's court. There, it's all bowing and praising and on and on. This is much better." Nergal dropped onto one of the stone benches. "Enki told me to come here and soothe your wounded pride. Do you feel better now that I've come all this way just because you stomped your pretty little foot and pouted with your lovely lips?"

I said nothing as I stepped down off the dais. Nergal's green eyes tracked my every motion. I walked slowly toward him, allowing his gaze to slide over my body. He made no effort to hide his lust.

"You must be weary from your travels, and I have not even offered you refreshment. As you say, we are not much on ceremony or comfort here, but that does not mean we have nothing to offer." I let my words hang in the air, ripe with the obvious double meaning.

Nergal grinned wickedly and excitement lit his eyes as he once again perused my body with his gaze.

"What can I get for the God of War? Wine? Bread?" I sat beside him on the bench. My shoulder brushed against his as I turned my head to face him. Close enough to kiss, I gazed into those haughty green eyes and heat licked through my stomach.

"You seem familiar," Nergal murmured.

I thought of our conversation on the terrace under the stars, but decided not to enlighten him. He leaned toward me, studying my features.

"Perhaps you would like to wash your feet or rest? I've had chambers prepared for you." My voice sounded breathy and excited.

"I'm not staying." Nergal jerked away, breaking the spell. He stood and frowned down at me. "Why would I want to stay here?"

His insult reminded me of my objective. I'd gotten lost in my attraction. Angry, mainly with myself, I stood toe to toe with him.

"You will leave when I give my permission to leave."

Nergal's brows shot up and he threw his head back and laughed. It echoed in the empty chamber. He bent over at the waist, overwhelmed in his mirth.

I waited as white-hot fury built in my breast. His arrogance would be his undoing.

Finally, he straightened and gave me one of his heart-stopping grins. It only added to the rage pounding through me. When he raised his gaze to mine, he said, "I ask permission of no one." He bit out the words as he crossed his arms over his chest and raised his chin defiantly, challenging me to prove him otherwise.

At a head taller than me, I had to look up to meet his

eye. He met my gaze without a flicker of doubt about his claim. A smile froze on my lips, and I let death rise to the surface. The grin faded from his lips as I grew to tower over him. He tried to look away from the empty void of my eyes and the decaying flesh of my face, but I snared his chin in my bony claw and forced him to face me.

"I am Ereshkigal. I am the infinity of death. I am the end and the beginning." The strength of Irkalla swelled within me, but the God of War, recovered from his initial shock, rose to meet me.

Nergal challenged me, knocking my hand away. The aggression of war and destruction slammed against me, pounding me with the fury of his anger.

"I am Nergal, the destructor, Nergal the conqueror, Nergal the avenger. I have no weakness and know no fear." His green eyes flashed with power and dominance.

His hand fisted my hair. He held my face inches away from his. I gripped the front of his robes and pulled him toward me with equal force. Silence echoed through the hall after his words as we stood locked together, neither willing to back down.

"Bow," I demanded through gritted teeth.

Nergal narrowed his eyes. "I do not fear you, Lady Death," he murmured, tightening his hand in my hair.

Our conversation on the terrace replayed in my mind.

She is a constant companion on the battlefield.

"Do you think you know me? Have you seen me haunting the field of battle and think I will never point to you?" I whispered, pulling him closer. I was the goddess once again, flesh and beauty restored.

Nergal sucked in a breath at the contact of my body against his. He loosened his hold on my hair as he studied my face.

"I know Irkalla has nothing to fear for me. Take me or not." Nergal lowered his face to mine. I shivered as he whispered his next words against my ear. "I am the greatest warrior the world has ever known. You will welcome me to your hall and seat me at your right hand." His arm slipped around my back, anchoring me to him.

My simmering passion boiled over, tangling with my fury at his disrespect. His lean, powerful body pressed against mine, and my head spun with desire. His words held truth. Should he ever fall in battle, his honored place in Irkalla was assured, but his arrogance would not do.

I turned my face and the God of War smirked with confidence that he had won. My answering smile dripped honey as I sunk my fingers into his thick black hair. I closed my fist, twisting. Nergal's smirk tightened, but he refused to acknowledge any discomfort. I brushed my lips against his before skimming kisses along his jaw and pulling his ear to my mouth.

I whispered, "In the presence of Death, a warrior should be above all else...," I paused, sighing against his neck as his hands roamed over me. "Humble." I breathed the word and Nergal's hands froze.

I released my mounting anger and driving lust in a sudden blast of fury. Nergal's eyes widened in surprise as the wails of the dead rose around us. At my unspoken command, they surrounded him in a cyclone of desperation. The God of War rose into the air, his hair whipping around his face as the winds of death tossed and tumbled him in their grip.

I raised my hand, recalling the storm. As suddenly as it appeared, the winds stilled and Nergal fell to the stone where he lay face down, unmoving. I waited. Slowly, he rolled to his back and took a deep, shuddering breath. He stared unblinking into the blackness that shrouded the great hall.

I looked at the god, fallen, vulnerable before me. An inferno of desire raged within me. I hurried to him and lowered my body over his with my knees on either side of his hips. Leaning forward, I pressed my breasts against him as I claimed his mouth. Gently, I teased his lips apart, tasting him deeper and with growing hunger. His arousal pressed against my core, and I rocked against it.

Nergal's gaze locked with mine as I moved over him, pleasuring myself, feeding the beast of desire that rampaged within me. Lust and anger warred in his eyes as his body responded to my call.

The torches crackled as the flames jumped and danced. Nergal bucked and squirmed beneath me as I continued to grind against him. His hands roamed over me, tearing away my robes to expose my breasts. His touch, far from a gentle caress, sent shivers through me while erotic heat bloomed in my core. Never had I felt pleasure as intense as what Nergal stirred within me. Mindlessly, I rode the rising tide, moving with no other goal than to chase that which beckoned me. My eyes drifted closed as I surrendered myself to the wave of bliss.

Nergal timed his strategy perfectly. In one powerful movement, he shifted and rolled, pinning me beneath him. Cold stone greeted my bare back and my breath caught. I struggled to escape, realizing too late that I had lost control, lost my focus.

I coiled the energy of the realm within me as I pushed against Nergal's shoulders, trying to shift his weight. His mouth found mine in a brutal kiss that stole my breath and my wits. The surge of energy meant to repel him slipped away as I moaned and opened myself to him. His breathing came in ragged gasps as he kissed and nipped down my neck. I rocked my hips up, desperate for the release that was close.

Suddenly, Nergal sat back on his heels, still astride my hips. He threw his head back and laughed. I felt his power, wild and excited, swirling around him as he shook with laughter.

I froze, insulted rage boiling within me. He would burn in the deepest pit of Irkalla for daring to laugh at me.

Vengeful power roared in my ears, but before I could lay waste to the God of War, he cupped my face with his hand. His thumb ran over my lower lip, and he looked down with exquisite tenderness. Those green eyes that had haunted me burned with admiration and desire. His hair fell over his forehead, and I reached up to tuck it back. He turned his face into my hand and kissed my palm.

"So little surprises me. I believe Irkalla's charms are growing on me," Nergal murmured as he lowered his mouth to claim mine.

He shattered me with that kiss. No aggression, no power struggle, just sheer desire—for me the goddess, the queen, the woman on the terrace. His kiss asked for all of me, for the God of War accepted nothing less. He wanted me, needed me, and he offered the promise of pleasure beyond my knowing. His power flowed with mine, twining together until the very foundation of Irkalla shook beneath our building need.

I abandoned myself to him, desperate for what he offered. I answered his kiss with all my passion, letting the fire within me rage out of control. Nergal touched, tasted, explored my body until I shook with desire. My skin ran with sweat, and my core drew tight.

Nergal took his time, holding me in that sweet torture,

but ultimately, his need overwhelmed him. He moaned low and feral as he claimed me. Fire filled the hall as our climax reached its fevered peak.

Brilliant colors danced in my mind as Nergal and I became one. The intensity of our combined power reverberated through the realm and the dead danced in answer to the storm sweeping over them. Irkalla blazed with light as I flew apart in Nergal's embrace.

Utter stillness followed our climax. Only our ragged breathing broke the silence. Nergal's forehead rested against my shoulder and his weight pressed me against the stone floor. I couldn't summon the will or energy to care. I drifted, not completely tethered to my body. I was in a place between, feeling the aftershocks of pleasure and the rustling of the host.

The Great Bull never drove me to the heights of ecstasy like Nergal did. A considerate lover, the Bull had been gentle and deferential, as was his nature. I never knew anything like what just happened was even possible, but now that I tasted it, I wanted more.

My hands slid up and down Nergal's back. His bronzed skin was slick with sweat and reflected the torch light that flickered. I moved restlessly beneath him. He laughed low in his chest and pressed a kiss to my shoulder.

"You want more, don't you?" Nergal whispered the question as he nibbled at the base of my neck.

I wrapped my legs around him and rocked my hips in response. He growled against the hollow of my throat, a primal sound that made my grip tighten and back arch. He sucked in a breath and let it out, pushing away from me to stand. He bent and scooped me up in his arms.

"You will get all you want, greedy queen." Nergal kissed me as he stalked out of the hall.

CHAPTER TWELVE

We didn't leave my chambers for a very long time.

"Your skin feels like a polished stone," Nergal murmured as he slid his hand up and down my back.

I curled against him with my head on his shoulder, tracing a light pattern of circles across his chest. I had lost all track of time since Nergal had tossed me unceremoniously on my bed and taken me in another firestorm of uncontrolled lust. Our passion drove us onward, and we had reveled in our pleasures.

Finally, with our hunger for each other sated, we rested.

"Would you like a bath?" I asked, propping myself up on my elbow and looking down at him. I pushed the hair off his forehead with a smile.

Nergal drew in a long, contented breath before letting it out with a sigh. His eyelids drooped drowsily, and he stretched like a fat, satisfied cat.

"That sounds wonderful. Will you join me in it?" His hand closed around my breast and his thumb slid over my nipple making it draw tight. My toes curled in pleasure, and I shivered.

"Most definitely," I promised. I slipped off the bed and pulled on my robes as Nergal rolled to his side, his eyes drifting closed. I opened the door and called for a bath.

Jaz stood outside the door. Her expression froze in neutral indifference, but I could see the disapproval in her eyes. I didn't care. I didn't need her approval. However, I couldn't bring myself to shut the door in her face without at least saying something. But I didn't know what to say, so I waited, knowing Jaz's impatience wouldn't let the silence last for long.

"It's been seven days," Jaz said, crossing her arms over her chest. She flicked her gaze over my shoulder to where Nergal lay dozing on the bed. "Has he bowed?" She got right to the point.

With that one question, Jaz punctured my blissful haze. I left Nergal sleeping and closed the door behind me. Jaz fell into step with me as we walked down the dark tunnel.

"No." I clipped the word out and refused to offer more.

Jaz wouldn't care in the last seven days—Mother Goddess, seven whole days—I had felt more, experienced more, than I had in the centuries before. Nergal filled me with color and wonder. We talked as we touched, and he told me stories. The God of War, arrogant and insolent beyond measure, was also a keen observer with a quick wit and profound tenderness when he wanted to show it. He made me laugh and knew exactly how to make me tremble with desire.

We walked in silence for a moment, but as I knew she would, Jaz pressed the issue. "He must bow. He cannot stay without acknowledging your authority."

"He will bow when he is ready," I replied and put an edge to the words, hoping Jaz would let it go.

"He should bow when you command," Jaz snapped.

Demons were tenacious creatures. I smiled, thinking of the past seven days. He had done my bidding, and I his, with glorious results. I didn't care if it took him a millennium to bow. We would spend the time wisely.

"He will—"

An ear-splitting wail cut off the rest of my comment. Someone had breached the gates. Jaz spun around, sprinting toward the great staircase.

Slower than my demon guardian, I arrived several moments after Jaz. I stumbled to a stop beside her and looked around in horror. Sunlight spilled down from the world above. All seven gates stood open, hanging crookedly on their hinges. The bodies of the demon sentinels lay crumpled by the gates they failed to protect. Other demons swarmed the area, picking up their fallen comrades and taking up their posts.

Jaz yelled a volley of orders, though it seemed everyone was already doing what they needed to do. A shock of white hair caught my eye. Neti shoved his way through the seething mass of demons, shades, and shadows. His lips pressed together, and his eyes burned with fury.

"What happened?" Jaz snapped as the gate keeper approached.

"That filthy mongrel son of a goat broke through the gates. The demon gallas sent by the One Who Knows aided his flight. Riding the chair from above and shrieking with laughter, the God of War escaped. Lord Namtar followed in pursuit." Neti fell to his knees. "End me, my queen. I cannot exist with this shame of failure."

The chair. Mother Goddess, how did I not think of it?

Enki wove magic within the chair to provide Nergal safe passage to and from the Underworld, allowing him to escape the rules that balanced the realms. As long as he rode the chair woven with my hair, he was exempt from the law that claimed any who crossed to Irkalla could not leave without a soul to take their place. They played me for a fool.

Pain lanced through my heart as fury consumed me. The God of War, expert strategist, had executed his plan perfectly. I looked around the chaos of my domain. Shadows streamed through the open gates and tremors rocked the foundations as darkness escaped through the open boundaries, skewing the balance between the realms.

Shame and anger flowed through me as I sealed the gates. One by one, they righted themselves in their frames and slammed shut. Seven thunderous crashes echoed, each one breaking my heart into smaller pieces of stone, until only dust remained.

Darkness clouded my vision as I let power surge through me unchecked. The world shook as the gates closed. I imagined the fear surging through the heavenly court as the Earth quaked and bucked. Let them worry, for they had cause to be concerned. Reverberations rolled through the kingdom fed by my displeasure.

Jaz's hand gripped my forearm. "Stop this. Focus your anger on the one who deserves it. You'll tear the world apart if you do not harness your emotions."

With an effort, I stopped the flow of cataclysmic power and looked down at Neti. Anger snapped and crackled like a flame, but I didn't release it. Neti wasn't the one who deserved it.

"I would not end a faithful steward of the realm. Rise, Neti. I underestimated the God of War and the One Who

Knows. It is not your fault; it is mine. Go back to your post and send teams out to retrieve those who have escaped."

The gatekeeper got to his feet. With a miserable expression, he bowed once again to me before turning and trudging up the stairs to his station at the main gate.

"Nergal has much to answer for," I growled.

"Is your vision cleared of your lust? Can you see his trickery and cunning?" Jaz demanded.

"Yes," I snapped, though my heart gave another painful throb, thinking of his betrayal. I pushed past the demon and started up the stairs. "I'm going to inspect the gates."

Jaz wisely didn't follow.

CHAPTER THIRTEEN

As I climbed the endless staircase that rose into the blackness, I carefully stoked the flames of my wrath. Nergal's manipulation cut me to the core. I wondered if any of the tenderness or the words he whispered in the dark had meant anything. Had it all been an act, a sham, so he could escape and humiliate me in the process?

Shame and self-loathing crawled through me. With every step, I despised myself more. Rage at Nergal's arrogance and audacity mingled with anger at my own stupidity until I shook with the effort of containing it. I climbed methodically, the gates swinging open at my command and the demons bowing with no acknowledgement from me.

I tripped near the top and the crack of stone against my knees and hands jarred me out of my mindless journey. Beneath me, someone squeaked as I fell on top of him. Not a shade of the dead. This man was among the living.

I scrambled away from him and gasped in surprise as I recognized my father's messenger, Belanum, huddling on the stairs. His black hair now clung to his scalp in clumps of white and his flesh hung on his bones like an oversized robe. He looked at me with wild eyes for a moment before he resumed his crawling progress up the stairs.

The main gate was in view and Neti stood glowering down at the pitiful creature, who clawed his way toward the land of the light. A sharp blow to the gate behind him made Neti whirl around, pulling a massive, curved blade.

"Neti! Open the gate!" Namtar's voice carried through the stone barrier.

Neti didn't sheath his sword but opened the gate a crack to peer through. When he pulled the stone aside further, Namtar pushed through the opening and hurtled down the stairs, only to stumble to a stop a moment later as he met me and Belanum.

"Mother. I have news." Namtar paused for a moment and pulled in a deep breath. Judging by his flushed cheeks and heaving chest, he'd run from wherever he'd come from. His words came out in a rush.

"I followed that filthy dog all the way to the heavenly court. The galla Enki made for him blocked me from entering. I petitioned Shamash to help me, and he turned his glare on them until they melted into piles of mud. I crashed through the gates with my blade drawn and demanded Nergal show himself. The whole heavenly assembly stared at me like I'd gone mad. They said that Nergal had flown through the court moments before but was no longer there. Enki invited me to look through the assembly." Namtar's mouth pressed together in an angry line. "I looked into the eyes of every god, goddess, and servant in that palace and not one was Nergal. I have no idea how he escaped me."

Namtar sat down on the stairs with a disgusted sigh and looked up at me, despondent and angry. I considered his story, trying to think of what trick the clever Enki would have played.

"It's not your fault, Namtar. Enki, the Wise One, is a master at deception and Nergal's cunning knows no bounds." I sighed and sat down next to my son. He leaned against me, still warm from his exertions and the sun.

Belanum gained another step and halted as he encountered our feet. He looked up at us with bleary eyes and mumbled something.

"Poor creature," I murmured. "I wish I had never laid eyes on him."

Namtar nodded glumly and hung his head.

A fresh round of anger swelled in me as I considered the humiliation Nergal brought to my realm. I would not stand for it and Enki needed to learn he had no power over Irkalla.

"Namtar, was there anyone who you did not recognize as you searched the court? Anyone you have never seen or seemed out of place?"

Namtar's brows drew together as he considered. "I have spent little time in the heavenly court, so there are many there who are unfamiliar to me. But there was one old man who sat among the assembly, and I remember thinking he looked strange. He had a hunched back like a beggar but wore tasseled robes. I've never seen him before, but as I said, that means little. He bowed with everyone else when Enki commanded it." Namtar shrugged. "I don't know mother. Maybe Nergal just blew through the court to escape my pursuit."

"Perhaps," I murmured as I considered what he said.

My time with Nergal had not been spent entirely in carnal bliss. We talked a lot and while his betrayal caused me to question every moment, every whisper, I believed I learned at least a little bit about the true Nergal. He would not run and cower behind the court. He had been there, in plain sight. I was sure of it.

"Belanum, messenger of the great Anu, I'm afraid you'll need to stay as our guest a while longer, but I promise your rewards will be great when you come to Irkalla to stay," I said, addressing the pitiful man at my feet as I stood and hurried toward the main gate.

"Mother, what are you doing?" Namtar demanded, scrambling to catch up with me.

"I am going to see for myself." The massive gate opened at my command. "Neti, Belanum may not leave until I return, but do what you can to ease him." Neti nodded and flicked a glance down to where Belanum made his slow way toward the top of the stairs.

Namtar followed me through the gate. I rearranged my robes to hide my skin and hurried to Hulla's door. I didn't knock in my haste to get out of the sun and startled the poor woman as she rested next to the low burning fire. She jumped to her feet and, realizing who I was, dropped to her knees.

"Rise, Hulla. I need your help once more."

Hulla, Mother Goddess bless her stalwart nature, rose to the challenge. She asked no questions and rushed to barter for a beggar's cloak when I told her of my need. In exchange for a sack of barley, she traded with a traveler on the road and returned with a ratty cloak.

"The greedy son of a pig," she groused as she shook it out, wrinkling her nose at the odor. Made from the roughest cloth I'd ever seen, the cloak smelled like a musty goat pen. "I'm sorry, my lady. This is the best I could find, though I paid three times what it's worth." Her indignation at the poor deal made me smile despite my agitation.

"No matter. It will serve." I transformed from a goddess to an old, hunch backed woman and pulled the cloak over my gray robes.

Hulla's hands trembled as she held the polished silver mirror for me to survey my new appearance. I stared at the skin that hung loosely around my face. Deep wrinkles creased my skin and my white hair lost its luster. Nothing remained of me, save my eyes that danced with flames.

I took a steadying breath and closed my eyes. Like a fist unclenching, I let go of my anger, shame, and embarrassment. I found my center and settled myself in detached resolve to see my plan through. When I opened my eyes, the rheumy eyes of the elderly stared back at me.

Hulla gave me a weak smile. "I would not know you, my queen."

I nodded. "Good. Let's hope I can fool the court as well. If nothing else, the stench will keep them at a distance."

"Good luck," Hulla called after me as I left her as abruptly as I had intruded.

I didn't spare the heavenly gate a second glance as I slipped around to a side entrance. Even on a day with no feast, a steady stream of people visited the palace, seeking blessings, bringing news or goods, or asking for arbitration with issues. I shuffled along with my hunched back and stinking cloak. Most people ignored me, an old crone coming to beg for a blessing. Once in the palace, I sat on the edge of a burbling fountain and, from under my hood, surveyed the assembly.

The hall sparkled as it had on my previous visit, but the atmosphere was one of boredom and routine. Only a handful of servants circled the room offering refreshments. Clusters of men gathered around tables or stood along the side of the room waiting for their turn. Anu, Ishtar,

Shamash, and Enki sat on a raised dais and counseled with a small group of merchants complaining about thieves in the marketplace. Of course, Nergal was nowhere in sight.

I observed the court as I searched for any sign of the God of War or the elderly man who Namtar mentioned. The court flowed around me, chattering, gossiping, and whining about their trials and tribulations. Nergal hadn't exaggerated the tediousness of it all. I sighed and tapped my toe, impatient with their petty worries and needs.

Namtar arrived moments later. Without an official proclamation, no one stirred or bowed, for today he was just a minor god among many older, more powerful gods. He nodded to a few of the gods as he walked among them, looking for the old man.

"Are you looking for someone?" Enki joined Namtar as they wound through the clusters of gods and men.

"That old man from before. I cannot help but think you have tricked me, Wise One." Namtar glared at Enki and raised his eyebrows in question.

Enki nodded with an aggrieved expression. "Your mother distrusts me and I cannot blame her, for I helped Nergal escape. He was never meant to stay in Irkalla. I sent him to make amends, nothing more. I should have realized the God of War plays by his own rules and does not follow directions." Enki's tone turned bitter, and he pressed his lips together in aggravation before he continued, "However, I do not know of this old man you seek."

Namtar's expression mirrored Enki's annoyance, but he didn't openly challenge the claim. He knew his place among the court. Enki clapped him on the shoulder and called for some refreshment, clearly hoping they had settled the matter. Namtar flicked a glance at me as Enki steered him to a seat on the dais. A servant appeared with wine and bread, and Namtar accepted the refreshment automatically as he continued to survey the assembly.

The merchants finished their business on the dais, but instead of calling the next person forward, Enki asked, "It has been a dull day. Is there no one with a story?"

My suspicions rose. Enki was the most renowned storyteller in all the realms. Gugalanna often carried his tales to the Underworld and told them for the host's enjoyment. If Enki wanted a story told, why did he not tell it himself?

A ripple of interest rolled through the assembly. Stories and songs were their favorite diversions. Though I still simmered with rage, I hoped someone would step forward with entertainment. I worried my journey had been in vain. Perhaps Nergal had simply passed through the court and if that was the case, he could be anywhere under Anu's heavens by now. If someone offered a story, at least then I would have gained something for all this trouble. I jumped when a familiar voice rang out behind me.

"I have a story, Enki." Nergal made his way through the whispering crowd.

I doubted he offered to tell stories for the court very often, considering his disdain for his fellow gods. I pulled my hood further over my head as Nergal passed me, but he didn't give me a second glance. He sauntered past as if he was the Great Father himself.

"Lord Nergal, this is unexpected," Enki's voice carried a clear warning. He didn't seem happy to see the God of War.

Namtar sat up straighter in his chair and made to stand, but Enki caught his arm. Namtar relaxed back into his chair, shooting a furious glare at Nergal, who completely ignored him.

"I have recently had an adventure," Nergal began.

My blood ran cold. If he told the assembly about his trip

to Irkalla, they would see us as weak, conquerable. Frantically, I looked at Namtar. He must stop this before Nergal made us look like fools. Namtar's expression shifted to murderous as Enki once again restrained him.

"But that is not the story I wish to tell today. It will become legend soon enough, but it puts me in the mood for a story about a courageous, cunning warrior who none could best." Nergal paused and looked around the room, ensuring all attention was on him. Namtar jerked his arm away from Enki and sat glowering at Nergal's back.

Nergal launched into the well-known tale of King Gilgamesh and his epic adventure with his faithful companion Enkidu to the Cedar Forest. My stomach clenched as Nergal retold the tale of how they outsmarted the demon Humbaba and carried away a great cedar for the door to Gilgamesh's palace in Uruk. Gilgamesh killed my husband. Icy fury rolled through me as Nergal glorified the pair as great warriors, though they would never be anything but murderers to me. I trembled as I pressed my lips together over the scream that threatened to erupt.

On the backside of the wave of anger came crushing grief. In the whirlwind of recent events, my grief had gotten shoved aside, lost in a sea of new passion and discovery. Shame at my fickle soul and treacherous desires fed the fires of self-loathing that I carried after Nergal's humiliating departure. Not only had I allowed Nergal to make a mockery of me and my power, I'd forsaken the memory of my beloved Gugalanna.

Fresh heartache rose like a wound that refused to heal. I missed the Great Bull. His gentle kindness soothed me, and I longed to feel his peaceful presence as he cradled me to his chest like a precious treasure. I wrapped my arms around myself and tried to stop shaking, biting my lip as a tear slid down my face. I couldn't fall apart in the middle of the heavenly court.

Nergal's story drew to a close, and he looked around the crowd. Everyone sat in stunned silence before a general murmur of appreciation rose from the crowd. Nergal's gaze landed on me. With a frown, he moved with fluid graze and knelt before me.

"Mother, why do you cry?" the God of War whispered. His hand rested on my leg, and he pushed my hood back to see my face.

I swallowed hard against the grief that threatened to choke me but kept my disguise in place. I patted his hand where it rested on my leg. Age spots covered my ivory skin and my long, slender fingers bent with misshapen swollen joints.

"I am simply a weary old woman." My voice quavered with emotion. I sounded frail and feeble. Nergal's glittering green eyes filled with concern as he brushed away the tears from my cheeks.

My heart shattered. This was the man I had given myself to. This was the man who has spent days loving me and being loved by me. But he was also the insolent dog who used me, left me, and refused to bow his stiff neck. Great Goddess, why could he not just bow?

"Bring me a basin," Nergal called, and a stunned silence fell over the assembly as he slipped my sandals from my feet.

Namtar hurried over as a lovely young woman with a shapely figure and big brown eyes knelt next to Nergal carrying a basin of scented water. Namtar hovered behind her. She reached for my foot, but Nergal pulled the water to him.

"I will do it. Leave," he dismissed her without a glance

and picked up my foot. The girl scurried away with a surprised glance over her shoulder. The God of War washed each of my swollen, misshapen feet, gently massaging the old gnarled bones. His touch ignited a cascade of memories.

More tears spilled over as I tried to recall my anger, but only came back to the pleasure, passion, and tender love we shared. How could this man be the same as the haughty, arrogant god who taunted and mocked me in my own hall?

He dried my feet and slid them back into my sandals. Then, he turned to Namtar.

"Lord Namtar, I believe you have had a wearying day. Take your ease and let me refresh you."

Namtar's eyes widened, and a rustle of whispers ran through the assembly. Unable to refuse such an offer, Namtar sat stiffly and let Nergal wash his feet. When the God of War finished, he stood and shook out his robes.

"Thank you," Namtar said, with a curt nod to Nergal.

The God of War stooped and murmured near my ear. "Be easy, Mother. When it is your time, the Mistress of Darkness will welcome you in her hall."

I glanced uneasily at Nergal. Did he know who I was? His gaze gave nothing away. I said nothing but nodded my thanks and pulled my hood back to cover my face, hunching lower over my lap.

Nergal turned to my son. "Come, let us walk together. We have business to discuss."

Namtar hesitated only a moment before he fell into step with Nergal. As the two of them walked out of the court, I considered following. I dearly wanted to hear what they said, but Enki studied me with an uncomfortable intensity. It was time to return to Irkalla. I had duties to see to and needed to consider how best to deal with the God of War.

CHAPTER FOURTEEN

*N*amtar returned not long after me. I waited for him on my throne as the shades milled around the great hall. He hurried to me with a smile on his face.

"I have spoken to Lord Nergal. He will come to pay his respects to you soon." Namtar kissed my cheek and sat beside me. "We spoke at length. He regrets his actions. He was following Enki's orders and wants to see you again and apologize for his abrupt departure."

Hope and excitement blossomed within me. I smiled at Namtar and tried not to betray how happy the news made me.

"Just like that, the God of War plans to come in contrition to bow before a queen he insulted and discarded without a second thought?" Jaz's sardonic voice carried across the hall as she made her way to the dais, delivering a devastating blow to my euphoria.

Namtar stood and faced her with his eyes narrowed. "Nergal understands he does not want to be on the wrong side of Irkalla's power. He knows our queen is powerful, and he does not want her as an enemy. Besides, I think..." Namtar trailed off.

"What do you think? That he loves her?" Jaz took up her customary position behind me. "He knows nothing about love or loyalty or respect. He takes what he wants, as is his nature. He does not come to bow. He comes to make war."

My stomach churned as I listened to their argument. I wanted to believe Namtar. I wanted this confrontation done. If I were honest with myself, I wanted Nergal and I didn't care if he bowed or not. I despised this constant battle over respect and homage. I wanted the man who washed an old crone's feet and told stories to me in the dark. But I couldn't have one without the other.

"Ready the guards at the gates. Nergal is not to be interfered with. He may come or go as he pleases." I issued the order and took a deep breath.

We did not have long to wait. A demon brought the word that the God of War had once again presented himself at the gates. I forced myself to breathe as I waited. When the doors opened, Nergal walked through the hall with the same confident stride as always. He didn't look anywhere but at me as he made his way to the dais. I held my breath.

"I will speak to Ereshkigal alone," Nergal announced.

I nodded my agreement. "Leave us, please." The shades of the host left quietly. Namtar nodded at Nergal as he passed him. Jaz rested her hand on my shoulder for a moment before she stepped down from the dais.

"I know your heart, God of War. You will suffer tenfold what you give her," Jaz hissed low and angry as she stood nose to nose with Nergal.

Nergal gave her a bored look, ever the arrogant god. "When I am done here, you and I will settle our score."

Jaz stomped off, and I blew out a long, slow breath. Nergal returned his intense gaze to me, and the world shrunk to just the two of us.

Nergal pushed his hand through his hair, raking it out of his eyes. A smile tugged at my lips though I wanted to hold on to my anger. Jaz's words ran through my mind, but I couldn't bring my heart to believe them. Not when he stood there giving me one of his half grins. For a golden moment, I didn't care about respect or insults. I cared only that he was here with me again.

Unfortunately, the moment was fleeting and the rift between us demanded closure.

"Namtar tells me you have thought better of your insolence." I raised a brow while hope rose in my chest. Please let Jaz be wrong. Please let him bow so we could move past this.

His grin faded and his mouth twisted bitterly. "I regret that your son is a fool."

My hopes died in a storm of fury. Stiff necked man! Would he never yield? Could he not see what lay before him if he'd only bend this once?

I pushed to my feet, anger and wounded pride goading me on. "Your only regret will be coming back." I growled the words as power surged at my command, but Nergal charged forward and with a ruthless shove, pushed me back into my throne.

"My Queen, you have much to learn of war." He pinned my arms to the stone armrests of the throne as he lowered his mouth to mine, kissing me with vicious demand.

I turned my head, wrenching my mouth from his. He laughed low in his chest as I resolutely kept my face turned away from him. He pressed a kiss just behind my ear before he whispered, "Be still and listen to what I have to say."

"I refuse to listen to anything you say while you insult me and those in my house. Take your hands off me," I hissed back through gritted teeth.

Nergal let go of my arms and straightened but didn't back away. Refusing to sit looking up at him, I pushed to my feet, even though it brought me up against his unyielding body. He stood his ground, crowding me against the stone throne.

"Why did you come here?" I demanded. His body pressed against me, hot and beckoning. I wanted to touch him, taste him, and I despised myself for my weakness. I stood frozen with my hands curled into fists at my side and channeled my indignation into an inferno of hate.

"I wanted to make you an offer," Nergal replied as if he bartered for a cow, but I noticed his breath quickened and his eyes darkened with desire as my body pressed against him.

"There is only one thing I want from you," I said, pleased my voice stayed steady despite my hammering heart.

"Only one?" Nergal asked, pressing his hard cock against me, and slipping his hand into my robes to tease my breast.

I swallowed and wrestled against my body's response.

"Get on with it. Bow so I can take my pleasure with you again or feel my wrath for I have no more patience for your insolence." The trembling of my body diminished my grand proclamation.

"Then we are of the same mind. I will take you as a wife and be your king. Then, our pleasure will know no bounds and our combined power will be unstoppable." He opened my robes, baring my breasts to his hungry mouth. He suckled eagerly as he opened his own robes to free his hard, throbbing cock.

My heart hammered as my head spun. Pleasure and heat whipped high and hot within me, but his words penetrated the pulsing need that had me panting and quaking in his arms. He wanted to be my king, to rule my kingdom. He did not offer to rule beside me, acknowledging my sovereignty. He sought to take it all away.

I closed my hand around his cock and squeezed. He groaned and thrust into my hand. I tightened my grip, and he bucked harder, closing his teeth brutally on my nipple. Holding fast to my rage and indignation, I squeezed as hard as I could, pouring my power into my grip. His howl of rage shook the walls. I ducked away from his backhanded blow and let him go with a disgusted shove. He stumbled back off the dais and sprawled ungracefully at my feet.

For a moment, I thought he might bow. He might see the potential of accepting me as a queen as opposed to trying to dominate me as a king, but his arrogance wouldn't allow him to do that. He pushed himself up from the stones and his green eyes held malice and rage.

"I see now where your son gets it. Perhaps it's all the time spent in the dark. It makes you stupid and blind. You'll regret this, for I will not offer it again. Next time I come through those gates; your throne is mine."

Nergal turned and stormed out of the Great Hall.

CHAPTER FIFTEEN

I retied my robes with shaking hands. Furious that I could feel anything for such a creature as the God of War, I pulled in a deep breath. I had to end this.

I ran into the dark tunnels. "Kur," I shouted as my feet pounded the stones. "I need you! Kur!"

In all my centuries in Irkalla, I never once voluntarily summoned my captor. I knew he would come to me, though. I heard footsteps behind me and recognized Jaz's heavy tread. Good. She needed to hear this as well.

I was about to shout again when the dim light of the tunnel flashed, and a hulking man stood before me. I skidded to a stop and waited for Jaz to catch up.

Mother Goddess, forgive me. I couldn't believe I was about to do this, but I needed all the power I could gather if I was going to stand a chance against the God of War.

"Does your offer still stand?" I asked Kur, whose golden eyes gleamed in the dim light.

Kur flashed a wicked grin. "Perhaps."

I ground my teeth together. A curse on all gods and

dragons. "I don't have time for games. I will marry you on one condition."

Jaz hissed behind me, but I held up my hand to silence her. Kur crossed his arms and leaned against the wall of the tunnel.

"You're in no position to make commands, my queen." He sneered at my title. "You need me."

My brittle control of my emotions snapped. I launched myself at him, slamming him back against the wall. His head met the stone with a crack. The power of death begged for release and I opened myself to its fury, letting it pour through me. I closed my skeletal hand around Kur's throat as his eyes blazed with golden fire. Growing ever more confident at wielding the immense power of the realm, I pressed down on my tormentor until I saw a tinge of fear flicker in his eyes. I pushed harder, stealing his breath with a crushing pressure. Kur's eyes widened and terror replaced fear. Satisfied, I released him, letting him slide down the wall and crumple at my feet.

"What is your condition?" Kur rasped, struggling to his feet.

"I will marry you. You will gain a seat at my table—and in my bed. You will be an advisor to the realm, but I alone am sovereign. Agreed?" I crossed my arms over my chest.

Kur rubbed his throat and frowned. After a moment's consideration, he dropped to his knees and bowed his head. "Agreed, my queen."

"Gather the shadow creatures and fire dwellers. Unleash every terror and abomination Irkalla has to offer. Our time in the darkness is over." My words echoed through the tunnels. They rumbled across the vast expanse of the realm. In answer, the host rose in unison with a cry of excitement and the surge in power made my head spin.

Kur pushed to his feet and swept me into his embrace. His heat unfurled around me as he kissed me with reckless passion. I answered his kiss, pushing away the echoes of Nergal's touch. The walls of Irkalla shook until he finally released me and stepped away. I pulled in a shaky breath as he regarded me for a long moment before disappearing into the darkness.

I stared into the shadows that swallowed him. I felt Jaz's disapproval and forced myself to face her. She said nothing as she stood still as stone, regarding me with a disappointed expression.

"You told me to use my power," I snapped as I pushed past her, heading back to Ganzir to begin our preparations.

Jaz didn't follow, but I heard her words in the darkness. "I told you to be a queen."

The palace was in an uproar as everyone scrambled to make preparations for battle. Namtar and Neti stood on the stairs of the palace, organizing troops into ranks and shouting orders. I joined them, carrying my armor.

Jaz materialized from the shadows, wearing full armor in all her demonic glory. She took the pieces from my arms. In silence, she strapped the breastplate on before wrapping my arms and lower legs in straps of thick leather. She slung my sword belt around my hips and adjusted it, so my weapon hung inline with my left leg before draping a heavy cloak made of linked bronze plates across my shoulders. Gloves made of supple leather with bronze guards that stood out in wicked spikes when I closed my fists protected my hands. She pulled the hardened leather cap over my silver braids and tacked a sheer veil across my face.

My heart hammered in anticipation. Despite the hours of combat training, I had never crossed swords with any other than Jaz, Neti, or Namtar. I couldn't find the words to tell how her badly I wanted to make her proud and be the warrior she trained me to be.

Her eyes glowed like red embers as she used her needle-sharp teeth to cut open her palm. She smeared her blood across my forehead and for a moment, her gaze bored into mine. I thought she would speak, offer me her blessing or words of counsel. Instead, she handed me my helmet and turned to face the host, standing shoulder to shoulder with me.

Her silence cut as deep as any sword, but she stood beside me. No matter what came, she would always be at my side. It gave me some solace. My stomach rolled with anxiety and unease, but I had made my choices. Everything was moving so quickly, and I wasn't at all confident with my choice, no matter what I said to Jaz. The catastrophic consequences ran through my mind and choked me with fear. How had it all come to this?

Jaz and I surveyed the endless sea of shadows, demons, shades, and creatures. They shifted and swayed with agitation.

Without looking at me, she murmured, "When you lead an army and ask them to fight with you, you must show no hesitation and believe without a doubt that you are in the right. They will follow you, Ereshkigal, for you are their queen."

I nodded and centered my thoughts, expelling the doubts from my mind. I had to protect the realm, my throne, and my heart. Concentrating on my rage, my wounded pride, and my broken heart, I refocused my conviction. Nergal must pay for his insults to my realm and there must be no doubt of the might and wrath of Irkalla.

Clinging to my conviction, I climbed the stairs toward the first gate with Jaz, Namtar, and Neti on my heels. We stopped halfway, just before the darkness engulfed the staircase when viewed from below. I breathed a calming breath, finding the warrior Jaz had taught me to be. Envisioning the outcome I sought, I exhaled and sent a prayer to the Mother Goddess and Anu that I would find victory.

I raised my arms and put my voice on the wind. "Warriors of Irkalla, hear me! Today we leave the shadows!"

Demons and furies shrieked their excitement while the shades wailed and hissed. In the distance, I saw the fearsome fire dwellers' flames dance with anticipation. Creatures without name added their voices with a thunderous roar and the foundations of the earth trembled. Their power pushed against the boundary between light and dark and their eagerness for freedom chilled me. They would lay waste to anything in their path.

Neti and Namtar stood silently beside me, keeping their own counsel, but Jaz offered one last chance to change my course.

"Do you really want to do this?"

My response rose instantaneously and without doubt, "I do. Nergal must pay."

The army of the dead, damned, and demonic shook the ground with their battle cry. Neti threw the gates wide open, and I channeled the power of the realm. I raised my hand, and with a vicious pull, ripped away the barrier between the living and the dead. In place for eons, it took more power than I anticipated, and I swayed on my feet. Namtar slipped his arm around my waist, but Jaz pushed him away.

"She will face the consequences of her actions on her own two feet. Stand up, Ereshkigal, Queen of the Dead, for the war you called for has begun."

CHAPTER SIXTEEN

I straightened my shoulders and glared at Jaz. The light streamed into the shadow realm. The shadows swallowed its heat and brightness. My army churned in their agitation, waiting for the call to surge forward into the land of the living.

With an echoing shout, I addressed the troops once again. "They think they are better than us, those who live in the sun. They think because they walk over us, we are beneath them. They doubt our strength. We will show them the wrath of Irkalla."

Again, the creatures responded with an ear-splitting cry, but a deafening roar echoed across the land, drowning the noise from the army. Fire filled the sky as Kur, in his dragon form, flew over the battleground. He landed before me with an earth-shaking thud. Flames poured from his mouth over the heads of the troops. Ecstatic enthusiasm answered the display, and I smiled up at my betrothed. Namtar and Jaz glowered at me, but I ignored them. I would show nothing but confidence in my course.

Kur coiled his body around me, and for once, I didn't

duck out of his embrace. His heat, intensified by his recent flames, engulfed me, making me sweat beneath my armor.

Kur's grating voice rolled through the kingdom as he announced, "Behold, creatures of Irkalla. I am your king and your creator!"

Frenzied with battle fever, the troops roared their reply. I shot Kur a warning look, unsure of where he planned to take this.

"Thank you for answering the call of your queen. They have insulted her, impugned her power and we cannot allow that to go unpunished. She needs our help! Today we defend her honor. Look to me for your orders and we will be victorious!"

Kur, manipulative, scheming beast that he was, knew these creatures respected strength. With a handful of words, he solidified his power and diminished mine. He claimed command of the army in battle—a right that I had not given him. His grip tightened on me as I squirmed, trying to break free of his constricting hold. With a clever shift of his body, he blocked me from view and roared, goading the troops into a frantic, churning maelstrom of flame and shadow.

Cold fury gripped me. I should have known better than to make an alliance with a creature who dealt only in lies and terror. I struggled against his ever-tightening grip, but Kur pinned my arms against me with his sinewy body. I shot a desperate glance at Jaz, but she kept her back to me, ignoring my struggle. Frustration and desperation swelled in equal measure as I twisted against the unyielding hold.

Be a queen.

Jaz's words echoed in my mind. A queen led through action. A queen sought to protect her realm and care for her citizens. My kingdom, made of spirits, shades, unwanted creatures of flame and shadow, was not the one I would have chosen, but it was my home, and they were my family. After eons in the darkness, I let go of the light. I let go of the resentment of the shadows with the epiphany that I had been the one making myself miserable for centuries.

I was Ereshkigal, Daughter of Anu, Queen of the Damned, and Unquestioned Ruler of Irkalla. Fueled by inspiration, I focused on who I was. No doubt, no fear, no regret crept in to weaken my claim. I knew myself for the first time and without any remorse for who I once was, I seized the power given to me by the ones who looked to me for guidance and protection. I would not let this creature torment them—or me—any longer.

I exploded out of Kur's grip. Icy blue fire filled me. I cast it over my realm with a sweep of my hand, extinguishing Kur's flames. A hush fell over the kingdom. Every creature held their breath as I faced the dragon. My tormenter, my betrothed, rose on his haunches to tower over me. I let his show of dominance go unanswered. He towered and postured while I cast my gaze over the sea of creatures until it landed on the fire dwellers. In the days of creation, Kur had banished them to the core of the earth to create the shadow realm and they had burned there, angry and vengeful ever since.

"I call to me the flames of the deep! Creatures older than the gods, hear me! Your King," I put a sneering emphasis on the title, "has kept you chained in the bowels of the earth. I understand now that power exists only so far as what we allow others to take." I pointed at the giant, looming beast. "He has no power over you unless you give it to him. I am queen and ruler of this realm. Kur, dragon of the deep, tyrant of Irkalla, you have no power over me or any creature who can hear my voice."

Uncertain rustling greeted my declaration. Kur's deep grating laughter cut through the silence, but I stood tall and confident as I waited.

In the distance, the fire dwellers shifted and swayed. Their flames snapped and danced as they absorbed my words and felt my conviction. In a blink, they grew from bright spots on the horizon to a raging inferno bearing down on where Kur and I stood. I smiled as their flames rolled over me with barely a tickle of warmth. Kur roared in defiance as they surrounded him in a fiery embrace. His roar disintegrated into pitiful shrieking as the creatures carried him away in their flaming claws, dragging him back to their pit of primordial fire.

Satisfaction settled in my belly as I watched. Jaz moved to stand beside me.

"You're learning, Ereshkigal. What now?"

I glanced at my demon friend. "Now, we teach the God of War a lesson in respect."

I rushed up the stairs to the first gate of Irkalla. It stood wide open, and I ran through it with Jaz, Namtar, and Neti right behind me. The shadows of the realm, no longer contained, spilled over and crept forward, swallowing the light as they went. I paused to face my troops once again.

"I am your queen, your sovereign, and your protector. I will lead you to glory for this day the shadow realm rises!"

Eager to get on with things, the ranks rose at my proclamation, screeching and roaring as they followed the shadows into the land of the living.

A rumble like distant thunder shook the earth. My breath caught as I saw the legions of warriors pouring across the land toward us. Nergal led the surge like the tip of a spear. His red chariot gleamed in the sun, pulled by two massive lions with deadly barbed scorpion tails. Endless ranks of soldiers flanked him, and several of the gods joined his side.

Ishtar's white helmet winked and glittered as she rode into battle on Nergal's right hand. The warrior god, Lulal, whipped his team of donkeys furiously as he entered the battlefield on Nergal's left. Above the advancing horde, the mighty Zababa flew on his eagle next to Imdugud, the terrifying abomination with a lion's head bearing a saw-like beak and wings big enough to blot out the sun. Every beat of his wings stirred the dust cloud of the oncoming army, camouflaging their numbers and armaments. My heart stuttered when I saw the fire god, Gibil, and Erra, the ruthless God of Violence and Pestilence, emerge from the throng to stand with Nergal. Their combined strength would challenge my warriors.

I took small comfort in the notable absence of Enki, Shamash, and Nabu, the God of Scribes, and several others of the heavenly host. As confident as I was in the might of Irkalla, the battle would cost even more dearly if more gods threw their lot in with Nergal.

The shadow army marched, slithered, and crawled forward. We had no flashy chariots to show our strength. A vanguard of shadows claimed the light, obscuring our ranks from Nergal's view. In our wake, flames trailed behind us, burning the sands and consuming everything in their path.

Namtar pointed to Hulla's hut, shuttered and silent. I nodded and cast a protective shadow over it and its mistress. Namtar smiled and straightened his shoulders. Together, we continued to the field of battle.

I marched onward with Jaz and Namtar on either side of me. Beside Namtar, the fearsome Ninazu stomped along, glaring around him. Snakes coiled around his body, undulating and weaving with his movements. Full of vengeance and forgiveness, his dual nature made Ninazu quarrelsome, and he traveled between the realms on a regular basis, rising and falling as was his nature. Today, he would rise and fall for Irkalla and I counted my blessings that he stood on our side. When full of vengeance, his thirst for victory was unquenchable.

Pazuzu, the son of Hanbi, God of Evil, rose from the shadowy flames and fell into step beside Jaz. Disturbing in appearance with his dog-like face, scaly skin, raptor talons, and a penis with the head of a snake, the demonic god was a welcome addition. His powerful wings could repel fire, disease, and curses.

Pazuzu brought Lamashtu with him, keeping her close on a tether with a metal collar around her neck. I shivered. Lamashtu haunted my nightmares with her long bloody fingers, each bearing a wickedly pointed nail. Her breasts swung bare as she walked on her bird feet with her lion's head alert and ready to strike. I was glad she was fighting at my side and not against me. Her thirst for blood knew no bounds.

My heart hammered against my ribs in a violent staccato. I kept my pace even and my chin up. These were my subjects, my responsibilities, my strength. Monstrous, dark, and dangerous, we were an army of nightmares, and we were coming to banish the light.

CHAPTER SEVENTEEN

The shadows led our march across the barren sands. I stopped our advance just beyond the reach of arrows and spears. Swords, axes, and shields in hand, my warriors waited patiently. Many trained in battle during their lives and even as a shade of their former selves, their discipline remained. The shadow creatures and wraiths hissed and rustled impatiently as the furies and demons kept a close watch on them, ready to pull them back if needed.

Nergal pulled up his army, unwilling to be the first to advance into weapon's range. The teeming mass of mortal warriors, demigods, creatures, and gods faced us across the wide expanse of barren sand. The walls of Eridu broke the flat line of the horizon, just visible through the haze of dust raised by Nergal's horde.

The world held its breath as the witnesses joined the field. From the shadow realm, the God of Justice, Enmesarra, and the scribe of the Underworld, Belet-Seri made their way between the armies. The noble Haya, God of Scribes, and the all-seeing Isimud with his double face joined them as representatives of the light. They would observe and record the deeds done this day. I straightened my shoulders and sent a silent prayer to the Mother Goddess that my actions would bring honor to my name and realm.

Tensions escalated as the observers took up their posts. The creatures of darkness stirred restlessly, and the mortal warriors' blood sung with the call to war. It was time.

I drew my sword which, like the rest of my battle gear, Jaz created in the depths of the earth. It sang its name as it left its sheath. Shargaz, the supreme smiter, sword of demons, death, and destruction, burned hot in my hand, answering my touch. The magic of the realm flowed through me, and flames burst to life along the sword's edge. Made for my hand alone, the weapon responded to my call. For anyone else, it was just a sword of the finest craftsmanship, but for me, one touch, one nick from the blade of death, and my opponent would incinerate from the inside out.

I held Shargaz over my head and the battle cry of the damned rose from my lips. "Eli Baltuti Ima'Idu Mituti- The Dead will outnumber the living. I unleash Death on the world!" Shargaz blazed silver white flames.

My troops thundered their approval, and I felt them coiled to spring behind me. All I had to do was flick my wrist and the army of the dead would swarm across the world. I wanted to. I felt the lure of power calling to me. Not only would I command the dead, the living would join my legions as the dead overwhelmed them. They would all pay for their sins of arrogance and conceit. They would know that their place in the light was only a fleeting moment compared to the eternity of darkness that was Irkalla.

For a heartbeat, I saw the world at my feet, felt the immensity of the power that I could command. But there was no light. Only gloom and shadow filled the universe. My thirst for power turned to dread as the inevitable conclusion of this conflict played out before me. The energy of my army goaded me forward, but the clarity of consequence restrained me. I would not have my name recorded as the one who stole the light from the world. I would not be the one who destroyed the balance of the universe over wounded pride and arrogance. There was only one way to prevent it and bend the stiff neck of the God of War, for he still had to pay for his disrespect of me and my realm.

Nergal answered my battle cry with one of his own, but before he could give the command to charge, I broke ranks, striding into the empty sand between the armies. My feet sunk into the shifting grains as I walked forward alone with Shargaz burning brightly in my hand. My troops fell in behind me, but I held my hand up to stop them.

"Nergal, God of Arrogance, God of War and Strife, come to me to settle this. Before the gods and man, we will fight and to the victor will go Irkalla with all its power." My voice carried across the sands, and I heard a rumble of shock ripple through both armies.

"I have bested you already, my queen." Nergal shot back his reply with a mocking inclination of his head.

I raised a brow and glanced behind me. "Forgive my confusion. I stand with the greatest army in creation at my back. If you have bested me already, why do they not answer to your command?"

The creatures behind me growled and bared their teeth. The demons and furies hissed and the wraiths' keening wails taunted out opponents.

Nergal threw his head back and laughed. "As always, you are as entertaining as you are lovely, Ereshkigal."

He spun and hopped out of his chariot. With long strides, he walked out to meet me, pulling his massive battle ax from the scabbard on his back. He twirled it expertly with a lazy rotation of his wrist. The soldiers standing in the light shouted their encouragement.

"If you want me to best you before all creation with scribes recording how I single handedly took the rule of Irkalla from its pretty little queen, by all means, let our blades cross here and now, though you ought to be careful with your little poker. You could cut yourself."

Nergal stood tall and proud in his armor, staring down his nose at me. His green eyes sharp and his unruly black hair sticking out from beneath his helmet. He wore bronze arm guards and a breast plate but did not carry a shield. He set his feet and held his axe at the ready with utter confidence in his position. My stomach clenched in the face of his power and my heart hurt remembering the tenderness he held hidden beneath his conceit.

I dropped my gaze and looked up at him through my lashes. "Nergal, God of my Heart, you are a fool," I whispered.

Nergal's eyes widened in surprise at my words, and I used the moment to make my move. I lunged forward, diving low, and came in under his late swing. I rolled to my feet, rising to stand nose to nose with him, inside his reach. Following my momentum like Jaz taught me, I threw myself against him, wrapping my arms and legs around him in a clinging embrace that took us both to the sand. Nergal twisted as we fell, so he landed on top of me, but I smiled up at him as he rocked back to strike me. I lifted my short sword that I had tucked between us and rested the tip against the underside of his chin.

"Careful, Nergal. You're correct that it's very sharp. You know this sword, do you not?" I asked, as Nergal froze in place and narrowed his eyes.

"I do." He bit the words out as he stayed as still as a statue.

"Will you bow?" I asked, hoping with all my soul he would say yes.

"I would rather burn a thousand deaths than bow to a queen who has no power over me." Rage twisted his features and those jade green eyes that made me melt with desire turned to ice with hatred.

"Oh, you arrogant fool," I sighed and pressed the tip against his skin. Tears blurred my vision and my heart shattered.

"Hold, Ereshkigal, my lost daughter, Queen of the Dead and Mistress of the Darkness. Lower your blade, for I am Anu and command it to be so!"

The command echoed across the land, and I froze at the sound of my father's voice. Nergal used the distraction to scramble away, hastily rubbing his hand over his throat. I pushed to my feet and turned to see Hulla leading Enki and Anu down the heavenly staircase.

Hulla's dark eyes filled with tears as she ran to me and fell at my feet, pressing her forehead to the sandy ground.

"My Queen. Forgive me, but I could not let you plunge the world into darkness. I begged the Great Father and the Wise One to intervene to save my people," Hulla raised her face and looked at me with earnest pleading as she paused before adding, "To save you."

Anger and relief warred within me. My vengeance and

unequivocal victory stolen, I wanted to shake the woman and tear her hair for interfering in a matter of the gods. Nergal still had not paid for his insults to me and my kingdom, and now it seemed he never would. But even as my pride stung, I sighed, grateful that I had not destroyed the man I loved. The thought of Nergal consumed by flames made my heart bleed with pain.

Namtar rushed toward Hulla's side, but I stopped him with a look. I bent down and pulled Hulla to her feet.

I wiped the tears and sand from her face and said with a voice that carried across the field, "You are a true daughter of Irkalla. Your bravery and loyalty shall be noted and your praises sung here after!"

My army sent up a cry of approval at my high praise and I kissed Hulla on each of her cheeks. In a softer tone, I added, "Thank you again, Hulla. You are worthy of my son, and I am proud to call you daughter."

I gave her a slight push toward Namtar. He wrapped her in his embrace, and I smiled with maternal tenderness and joy.

With a deep breath, I turned to face my father and brother. I bowed deeply to them, dropping onto a knee, and driving Shargaz into the ground. The flames on the blade died, and I studied the red sand beneath me as I waited for their chastisement.

From the corner of my eye, I saw Nergal bow with a jerky bend at the waist. Even to the Great Father, he struggled to abase himself.

"Rise, daughter. Embrace me, for it has been too long since I looked upon your face."

I leapt to my feet and, like a child, threw my arms around my father. In the early days of my banishment to Irkalla, I dreamed Anu would stoop down and scoop me up in his all encompassing reach. He would take me away from

Kur and his shadow realm and keep me close to him in the light. But as I grew up and learned the ways of the gods, I knew it would never happen. I gave up on the dream of ever seeing him again.

Anu's arms folded around me and for a moment, it was just me and him in all the world. He smiled down at me. For a heartbeat, I remembered what it had been like to be his daughter, full of light and life. I clung to him, happy to feel his embrace once more, but I no longer mourned the loss of that life.

"I have missed you, Ereshkigal, but you have done well with your responsibilities. Your realm is strong and you are an able mistress. No one, not I or any one on this field, doubt your power." His words reverberated across the sands. En masse, the armies dropped to their knees. I stared in wonder around me as every head bowed—except Anu's and Nergal's. I pressed my lips together in frustration. How could he still not bend his knee?

Anu squeezed my shoulder as he turned to face the lanky god as he stood leaning on his battle axe, looking disgustedly around him. The Great Father shook his head.

"Nergal, your talent for sowing discord is unmatched." Anu's dry tone suggested the statement wasn't a compliment. He gave a short laugh before continuing. "However, without discord, there would be no appreciation for peace. You are as necessary in this world as every other creature I have created."

Nergal gave Anu a bland look and said nothing.

Anu's lips titled in a slight smile before he continued, "I will not let you stir the world to war over your pride and arrogance. I decree, you will bow before your queen."

Nergal rolled his eyes and I wanted to strangle him for his insolence. "Not going to happen," he said and drew designs in the sand with the tip of his axe like he was bored.

Anu's lips pressed in a firm line. "One day, you will learn the strength in cooperation. From this day forward, Nergal, God of War, you will dwell in Irkalla under the rule of Ereshkigal, Queen of the Dead, for half of every year."

Nergal snapped to attention. His face flushed red with anger, and he grasped his axe, raising it to the ready. Enki rushed forward, and I pulled Shargaz from the ground, ready to defend my father. Anu raised a placating hand and Enki and I stood down, hovering nearby.

"You leave a wake of discontent wherever you go. We stand here today poised on the brink of battle because of your contrary nature. The world needs respite from you, Nergal. I am the Father of All. You will obey my command." Anu's words took on an edge, and he crossed his arms over his chest.

Like a cornered animal, Nergal's chest heaved as he sucked in breath after breath. If he chose not to obey, Anu would strike him down in a blink and replace him with another. I bit my lip and held my breath, hoping he would bend—just this once.

His gaze met mine. Rage and fury filled his green eyes. His natural tendency toward conflict combined with his pride stiffened his spine. They warred with his self-preservation. I pleaded silently with him to relent, to see the greater picture.

Nergal pulled the axe higher in the air. I tensed, but Anu didn't flinch. With a murderous swing, the God of War drove his blade into the sand and bowed his head.

"As you say, Mighty Father, God of All." The words came out in a strangled whisper.

With excruciating slowness, like every motion caused him pain, Nergal turned to me and dropped to his knees.

"My queen. I pledge my loyalty to you as your husband and will dwell under your rule as your father commands."

My heart broke as he removed his helmet and bowed his head. The haughty set of his shoulders dropped as he acknowledged me as his queen. Tears spilled over, coursing down my cheeks. I rested my hand on the back of his head, threading my fingers through his unruly black hair. His body trembled under my touch, and I felt no satisfaction at seeing a great warrior bend to the breaking point.

This would not do. I didn't want a broken warrior. I wanted a man who wanted me. I fell to my knees, joining him in his humility. In the sand between two armies, I lifted the face of the man I loved to look at me.

"By the command of the Great Anu, Father of All, I take you as my husband. I raise you to stand beside me, to rule with me, and be my equal in this and in all things." I stood, pulling him up with me. "Nergal, God of Arrogance, God of War, God of my Heart, will you stand beside me in the land of the dead, hand in hand, to lead the kingdom of darkness with a firm but fair judgement?"

My mouth went dry as I waited. His natural inclination to dominate and control fought with his oath and the promise I offered. Finally, he sighed and raked his black hair back off his forehead.

"Half the year," he growled in confirmation.

"Half the year," Anu echoed with a smile tugging at his lips.

"Do I have to let you out of the bedroom while I'm stuck in the dark?" Nergal whispered in my ear as he bent to sweep me up in his arms.

His kiss stole my answer.

The armies of the living and the dead raised their cheers to the heavens, but neither Nergal nor I heard them. He strode through the gates of Irkalla, down the stairs, and didn't pause until he kicked open the door to my bedroom and dropped me unceremoniously on my bed. He stood towering over me with a lopsided grin and his hands resting on his hips. His gaze roamed over me as he shrugged out of his armor and let it fall to the floor with a clatter.

Nergal laid beside me and pulled off my helmet and breast plate, taking a moment to mark the craftsmanship of each. He loosened my sword belt and tugged it free. With care, he set it beside the bed before pouncing on top of me with a swift motion. I stared up into his green eyes that burned with lust and something that I dared hoped ran deeper than desire.

"My wife." Nergal kissed me hard and deep, pressing me back into the blankets. "My goddess." He kissed my neck. "My Queen." He nipped my ear. "My Love." He sighed the words against my lips as he kissed me again.

I wrapped my arms around him. "Welcome home, husband, King of my Kingdom and God of my Heart."

ALSO BY A.C. DAWN

The Invisible Goddess (Myths Reimagined Book 1)
A Stranger's Kiss in Stranded: A Boys Behaving Badly Anthology
Crossing the Line in First Response: A Boys Behaving Anthology

ABOUT A.C. DAWN

A.C. Dawn is an active and enthusiastic author and reader of short stories, novellas, and novels. She enjoys bringing her characters to life and strives to stir the imagination of her readers. She believes the best writing touches the reader in ways they hadn't expected and will never forget!

So, that's the official bio...

Really, I'm a lover of chocolate, a strong jaw line with a 5 o'clock shadow, and romances that make your heart pound and your middle get all squishy. I love quiet country living on my north Georgia farm with my family and fur babies of all shapes and sizes. I think the scariest thing in life is how fast my daughter is growing and an empty coffee pot. I can't stand slow drivers in the fast lane and wimpy handshakes.

I have endless stories rumbling around among the rocks in my head. I can't wait to share them with you!

Want to keep up with me? Follow me here:

All the links here! https://linktr.ee/andycarley

Facebook Page: https://www.facebook.com/A-C-Dawn

Facebook Group: https://www.facebook.com/groups/chasingthedawn

Tiktok: https://www.tiktok.com/@acdawnauthor

Instagram: https://www.instagram.com/a.c.dawnauthor/

Bookbub: https://www.bookbub.com/authors/a-c-dawn

Amazon: https://www.amazon.com/~/e/B08711JGB4

Printed in Great Britain
by Amazon